"I've missed you so..."

Hunter's eyes were dark pools of yearning. "This is where you should have been, instead of on that damned tour. Here... in my arms." He began a slow, tortuous journey down her body with his hands, blazing a trail of molten desire, demanding an answering passion.

Gabby twisted her head, urgently seeking his lips. She swayed on her feet in passionate longing.

A deep shudder shook Hunter's large frame, and he wrapped his arms around her. "It isn't fair for one woman to be so exciting."

She gave a husky seductive laugh. "You're always trying to make love to me with your clothes on. Don't you think it would be easier without them?"

THE AUTHOR

When Marion Smith Collins was seven years old her prize-winning school essay was published in the local paper. "Since then," she admits, "the thrill of seeing my words on a printed page has never faded." After selling her first romance novel, Marion realized that her true vocation was romance writing.

"Now I've found my niche, my passion," she says. "I want to do this every day for the rest of my life."

Books by Marion Smith Collins

HARLEQUIN TEMPTATIONS
  5—BY MUTUAL CONSENT
 22—BY ANY OTHER NAME

These books may be available at your local bookseller.

By Any Other Name

MARION SMITH COLLINS

Harlequin Books

TORONTO • NEW YORK • LONDON
AMSTERDAM • PARIS • SYDNEY • HAMBURG
STOCKHOLM • ATHENS • TOKYO • MILAN

To Bob,
who has always given me a choice.

———————————◆———————————

Published August 1984

ISBN 0-373-25122-X

Printed in Canada

1

GABRIELLA CONSTANT toasted the broad, cashmere-clad shoulders with her wineglass. "Well, well, well. If it isn't the Great Hunter Graham."

He didn't even bother to turn around. "Hello, Gabby," he replied—his customary perfunctory greeting.

She wasn't annoyed by his indifference. On the contrary, the lack of notice produced a feeling of security that spurred her to further indiscretion. "I understand Graham House has a bestseller on its hands. A work of some depth, I'm told," she said with a slow, sly smile.

For a moment she wondered if he had heard. The noise level in the crowded room was not high, but she had spoken very softly.

Then the wide shoulders moved, shrugging, as though to dislodge a particularly annoying fly, but before he could turn, a middle-aged woman in pink jostled him. He steadied her ample form with a broad hand.

Vexed at the unknown woman, Gabby shoved the heavy-framed glasses farther up her nose with an impatient finger. She'd been about to get a rise out of the Great Hunter Graham—one of the few amusements that made these parties bearable.

"Oh, I'm so sorry," the woman murmured distractedly, and wiped at his sleeve with her napkin. "I've spilled wine on you."

"Only a drop," he assured her in his deep baritone. "No harm done." As he turned his head to smile down at the woman, Gabby was treated peripherally to the devastating effects of his well-known charm, and in spite of herself her heart responded with a slight acceleration.

Hunter Graham was probably six-five and as handsome as the devil himself. His hair was raven black and thick, just skimming the collar of his white shirt. The dark, intense eyes were the color of coffee, strong and rich when undiluted with cream. He was one of the few men that Gabby, at five-foot-ten, literally, if not figuratively, looked up to.

Hunter irritated her. She realized that she was no beauty, but he made her feel even more unfeminine, unattractive than she really was. Restless with the thought, she tucked a strand of hair back into her haphazard ponytail. Hunter's attitude toward her looks didn't matter today. It was his reaction to something far more important that had drawn her to this party.

Her reference to the Great Hunter Graham was only partially inspired by his size. His rugged good looks radiated the power and magnetism associated with success and wealth. But many men were wealthy and successful. Hunter also had that indefinable something, often called charisma or distinction by those trying to put a name to it.

Had the woman in pink been made of wax she would now be a small puddle at his feet, thought Gabby as she watched them. But at the woman's words, Gabby's ears perked up. "Congratulations,

Mr. Graham. I noticed that Lily Andore's book was still first on the bestseller list."

Hunter's smile widened to a grin. "For the second week," he acknowledged. "Thank you."

"And what about the elusive Lily?" the woman went on. "What's she like?"

Well-dressed men and women surged gently against them, but Gabby, unabashedly curious as to what his answer would be, edged around so she could see his face. She'd been waiting all afternoon for this.

Hunter gave Gabby a frown of annoyance for the intrusion before returning his attention to the pudgy woman. "I've been out of town. I'm afraid I haven't met her yet."

"Oh, yes. I'd heard that you had gone to the Far East to sign up that new husband-and-wife team who write intrigue. Hong Kong, wasn't it?"

"Singapore," Hunter corrected.

"Whatever," the woman said, dismissing Singapore and Hong Kong for the more interesting topic of their original conversation. "Some say you have your own mystery woman right here in Lily Andore," she prodded.

"I understand she's a charming woman, but unused to the glare of publicity, very retiring." Even Hunter seemed uncomfortable with his answer, and Gabby, who was sipping from her glass, choked, earning another frown from the black brows.

The woman gave a trilling laugh. "Oh, no, Mr. Graham. You can't get away with that! I've read the book." A pink sleeve fluttered as she fanned herself, "Whew! Hot stuff! And last week on that radio interview from Boston she said some rather scandalous things. Let me see if I can remember…something about Boston being the model for corruption in politics. That doesn't sound at all retiring."

Before Hunter could reply Gabby made her own escape through the crowd to a clear spot against the wall. She had heard enough for now. Breathing a sigh of relief, she slipped her feet out of the unaccustomed high-heeled shoes. She usually hated these parties, but this was one she wouldn't have missed for anything.

The "second Saturday soirées," as her mother liked to call them, had become a tradition in the comfortable Upper West Side brownstone. On the second Saturday afternoon of each month Henrietta Constant held an open house for "members of the profession."

To Gabby the phrase had always held a lot of wicked promise, but the profession to which her mother referred was the literary profession. Poets, biographers, historians, novelists, a few publishers and even an occasional editor gathered to talk shop in a strictly social atmosphere.

Over the years the parties had grown extremely popular and much too large, but Henrietta thrived on them. There were always the regulars, among them Admiral Sanders Hutton, U.S.N. (Ret.), who wrote the definitive history of the United States Navy and was now their neighbor; Willie Mortimer, who wrote that marvelous book about chess (he couldn't play worth a damn, but he certainly could write about it); poor Esther Thorpe, who once, long ago, had written a sweet book of etiquette for little girls and couldn't understand why her sales had fallen off.

Then there were the drop-ins—the celebrity authors, in New York for publicity or a contract negotiation, who tried to time their visits to coincide with Henrietta's open house.

A reluctant Gabby was often summoned to assist in the role of hostess. It wasn't that Gabby didn't like parties, and the guests were generally interesting, entertaining, charming. But more than once, when she'd met people she particularly wanted to talk to, she'd had the overwhelming urge to drag them out the door and down the stairs to her own street-level apartment. There it was quiet. There she could kick off her shoes, turn on the stereo to a background level and order a pizza.

Unbidden, her gaze returned to Hunter and the woman in pink. Would Hunter like pizza? He looked totally exasperated now, thought Gabby with wry amusement. The woman must be pushing for more information about Lily Andore.

She knew the gossip—indeed, it was a prime topic of conversation here in her mother's parlor—that Lily Andore, Graham House's newest author, was a woman of deep mystery, that Hunter Graham himself had never met her.

There was another school of speculation—that Hunter had pulled off the greatest publicity stunt of the year in not letting Lily Andore appear in public until everyone in America was talking about her. He would certainly be capable of that, if it were true.

Wouldn't they all be surprised to know there was someone in their midst who could tell them all about Lily Andore?

Hunter Graham had taken over a small regional publishing house upon the death of his father ten years ago, moved the whole operation to New York and built a national reputation through business acumen and brilliant marketing tactics. Now Graham House was one of the most respected houses in the business, but it hadn't risen to its position with a president who was bashful about publicity. Very few issues of any New York paper ever left the presses without at least a mention of Graham House, and Hunter and the beautiful women he often escorted were a favorite subject for the rotogravure.

Most of them were blondes, Gabby had noticed, and his dark-devil good looks were a perfect foil for a blonde. He hadn't brought a blonde today, though. She'd known as soon as he walked in the door that he was alone.

As her mother's publisher Hunter was always present at these functions. She had to credit him, Gabby admitted. He had kept on all the writers his father had published when Graham House was regional, even though he seldom realized much profit from their books. It would have been quite proper for Hunter to have terminated Henrietta's contract, along with several others, when his father died. She supposed he was lucky to break even on some of the more specialized categories.

"Gabby, darling?"

Her mother's light musical voice intruded on Gabby's thoughts. She turned her head to locate the source of the sound and with a silent groan slid her feet back into her shoes.

Henrietta was fluttering. One dainty hand patted her hair with a quick restless movement as she gave a distracted smile to a passing guest.

Gabby made her way through the crush of people,

neatly sidestepping an antique candle stand, to where Henrietta stood at the door of the dining room. "Everyone is having a lovely time, mother," she said with a reassuring smile when she finally reached her side.

"Do you really think so, dear?" her mother asked. Her eyes scanned the crowd impulsively. "I thought you invited Steven. Has he arrived?"

"No, mother."

"I like Steven," Henrietta confided impulsively.

That was an understatement if ever Gabby had heard one. She had been dating Steven Ward off and on for the past year. He was the principal of the school where she taught history. Her interest in him wasn't particularly romantic, but he was a favorite with her mother because of his rather stilted, courtly manner. They both belonged in another century. It was a shame that her mother was twenty years older, thought Gabby. Henrietta and Steven would have made a great pair.

Gabby grinned. "He said he'd try to be here, but I'm not sure where we'd put him. Either we'll have to move to a larger house, mother, or you'll be forced to make these gatherings by invitation only."

"We couldn't move from here, Gabby. It was your father's home. It wouldn't be easy to find another as convenient as this. You have your own separate little apartment and can walk to school." Henrietta spoke in her own endearing, flibbertigibbet way.

"I know, mother. I was only teasing." Gabby tried to interrupt the flow with amused frustration.

"Besides, this one is paid for," Henrietta added absently. Her mother's occasional lapse into practicality always amazed Gabby. She chuckled and shook her head.

Left a widow at a young age, Henrietta had never had to cut back on the standard of living she'd always enjoyed. Gabby didn't remember her father, but she was eternally grateful that he'd had the foresight to secure the future of his wife and daughter. They were not wealthy, but thanks to a trust fund or two they were comfortable. "Then perhaps we should enlarge the parlor," she suggested playfully.

Henrietta looked across the hall with a speculative glance. "It does seem to get more crowded every month, doesn't it?" She smiled up at her daughter. "Perhaps we should."

Gabby met the smile with a loving one of her own. Quite often she felt like the mother herself, rather than the daughter. Not only did she top Henrietta by a good eight inches, she was by far the more realistic of the two.

Henrietta was a dainty ladylike creature, pretty rather than beautiful, who never left her bedroom without being perfectly coiffed, made up and dressed; Gabby at her best was perpetually rumpled.

Slightly fey, Henrietta lived in a world that was as far removed from the bustle of New York City as the proverbial castle in the air, writing lovely little volumes of poetry and an occasional scholarly treatise on metrical composition. She was intelligent, but had an artist's quixotic outlook on life. Her books were always critically acclaimed, which made up in part for the fact that they were never commercially successful.

"Did you want me for something, mother?" Gabby reminded gently.

"Yes, dear." Henrietta turned to the buffet table behind her and picked up a small silver tray, which she handed to Gabby. "Would you please ask Mrs. James for more of the cheese puffs?"

"Sure." Gabby took the tray and threaded her way through the crowd to the kitchen. The door swung shut behind her, closing out all sound. The quiet was a pleasant relief. Even very polite, well-modulated voices grew quite loud when there were enough of them together in one house.

"More cheese puffs?" asked the housekeeper when Gabby proffered the tray.

"They always go first," said Gabby, smiling.

"How is it out there?" the older woman asked as she filled the tray with fresh pastries filled with golden yellow cheese.

"Crowded," Gabby complained, and sank into a chair while she waited. "Why do I agree to come to these things?" She tucked yet another escaping strand of dark brown hair into the unruly ponytail.

When Mrs. James smiled, her eyes crinkled at the corners. "Because your mother loves the two of you to share experiences. It gives her the illusion that you're alike."

Gabby laughed. "We may be close, but we're nothing alike, no matter what mother wants. She has only to look at me to see that."

Mrs. James's eyes swept over her white tailored blouse and unimaginative navy blue skirt. "Well... you *could* put on lipstick, Gabby," she said lovingly but with some sincere exasperation.

"I did," Gabby protested, her gaze impassive. "I must have eaten it off." She reached across the table to pop a hot cheese puff into her mouth.

"Is Mr. Graham here?"

"Mmm," Gabby hummed around the food, and made a face. After she'd swallowed she added sarcastically, "Yes, he's honored us with his presence."

Mrs. James lifted a brow. "Why are you so antagonistic toward him? He's always a perfect gentleman."

Gabby took another puff, and as she chewed she reflected on the housekeeper's words. Why? Mrs. James was right: Hunter was always polite even in the face of her barbs. Maybe that was why. It was almost as though he barely saw her, as though she weren't important enough to be angry with even when she provoked him. She should have grown used to his not taking her seriously. He'd been doing it for ten years now. When she remembered the way his eyes always just skimmed, never really looking at her, it made her angry. She'd seen the way he observed other women, slowly, taking in every detail, the brown eyes warming....

"Do you want him to notice you?" Mrs. James asked gently.

Gabby's eyes widened in alarm. "Of course not!" She definitely had good reason for not wanting him to notice her now. "He's just so damned pompous!" she added in what was a weak excuse for her reaction.

With a trace of sympathy, the older woman shook her head. "I don't think he's pompous at all. If you want him to notice you, Gabby, why don't you—"

"I don't!" she interrupted, and reached for the tray. "I *don't* want him to notice me." His attention would come soon enough, and when it came it would not be pleasant. Though Hunter had the demeanor of a gentleman she wasn't sure that, somewhere deep inside, there weren't the instincts of a more predatory beast. She was in just the position to bring out those instincts.

When Gabby returned to the dining room, her mother had been joined by Hunter. Gabby's step faltered for a moment, as often happens when one has been discussing another and suddenly sees him. He was smiling with affection at something Henrietta was saying.

Henrietta took the tray from her and placed it in precisely the spot where she wanted it. "Thank you, dear," she murmured. She fussed compulsively over the table, straightening a corner of the cloth, smoothing a wrinkle.

"Well, Gabby, how's school?" Hunter asked. Indignation at his supercilious tone straightened her spine. *Just exactly as though I were a pupil rather than the teacher,* she thought.

"Fine," she answered shortly, forcing down the temptation to make another saucy remark. Despite the frequent barbs she directed at Hunter, up close he was an intimidating presence. She reminded herself that she needed to be cautious. Still, his condescension was one step up from total indifference. Until two years ago *that* was all he'd ever shown her. She clamped her teeth together to keep from grinning at the memory of Hunter's face....

He had been named by an article in the tabloid *Exposé* as one of the fifty most eligible bachelors in America. Gabby had heard from her mother how furious he'd been. "Hunter would much rather be known for his prowess as a publisher than for his swinging life-style," Henrietta had told her. "Beautiful women go in and out of his life, but he's really married to that company."

Half in mischief, half in a desire to puncture his detached self-assurance, Gabby had clipped the article and waited until just the right time, an afternoon such as this.

Hunter had arrived with a beautiful woman— blonde, of course—on his arm. The crowd that Saturday had been smaller than today's, but a sufficient audience for her purpose. During a lull in the conversation Gabby had approached the handsome couple, her hand in the folds of her skirt. "I have something for you, Hunter," she'd said with a pretense at shyness.

He'd smiled down at her, and she'd almost lost her nerve under the force of his charm. "It's the clipping from *Exposé*." She'd withdrawn it from behind her, picture side up. "I was sure you would want it for your scrapbook."

The blonde had been impressed—she hadn't seen the article—which added to Gabby's enjoyment of the moment. The others standing nearby had tried unsuccessfully to hide their smiles.

She could still feel the quiver of fear that had struck her as Hunter's face suffused with red and his eyes narrowed dangerously. But he hadn't exploded, as she'd thought he would. Instead he'd calmly pocketed the paper she held out to him. "Thank you," he'd said in a tone that warned her of retribution at some future date.

Retribution had never come, however, and she had felt a grudging respect for his control, though seasoned with mild disappointment. It was a childish trick, she had to admit, looking back two years to the incident. She had been twenty-four then, certainly old enough to know better. She'd made herself apologize afterward. "Maybe being exposed to a daily dose of teenagers has had a worse effect than I realized," she'd told him with a nervous grin. "Certainly I know other teachers who experience burnout at an early age."

Hunter had treated her then to one of his slow, lazy appraisals. "I'd forgotten that you were a teacher. You barely look old enough to be out of school yourself."

She remembered quite clearly how inadequate she'd felt under his perusal, but at least he'd seemed to appreciate her apology.

From that time they had treated each other with tolerance if not friendliness. It was doubtful that they would ever be friends.

Gabby was drawn back to the present when she heard her mother ask Hunter about his trip

He stepped aside to let a guest pass before he answered. His shoulder brushed hers and Gabby was suddenly aware of his warmth. She wondered at her sensitivity to the brief contact. Could Mrs. James be right? Did she say outrageous things to him only to get his attention?

The housekeeper's head appeared around the door to the kitchen. She waved to attract Gabby's attention. "The phone's for you, Gabby," Mrs. James called out.

She hadn't even heard it ring. "Excuse me, mother, Hunter. It must be Steven."

"Steven?" Hunter's brow went up inquiringly.

"Gabby's boyfriend," explained Henrietta.

"Ah, the boyfriend," Hunter said with a dismissive accent on *boy*.

Gabby gave him a saccharine-sweet smile. "Yes. And I'm sure you're every *other* inch a gentleman." She whirled and left them.

Sassy brat, thought Hunter as he watched her go. How old was Henrietta's daughter now? Let's see... when his father died and he moved up to president of Graham, she must have been about...sixteen? That was ten years ago. No, that couldn't be right. Surely she wasn't that old.

He shrugged and promptly dismissed all speculation about Gabriella Constant's age. He had enough to think about. This damn Lily Andore thing! Not that he wasn't pleased; what publisher *wouldn't* be pleased with sales of eighty-five hundred in the first week? But, dammit, he didn't like to be in the dark. It was a hell of a time for Andore's editor to take a vacation! And the woman's agent had had her answering machine on for two days!

Hunter unbuttoned the jacket he wore and shoved his hands into the pockets of his trousers. He was tired. Jet lag, he guessed, just beginning to catch up. Plus the fact that he'd stayed awake all night on the plane reading Andore's book. He'd taken several advance copies with him, but hadn't got around to reading one—the writing team in Singapore had been particularly demanding—until after he'd talked to his office on the telephone just before starting home. And what a book it was! The woman had talent, an ability to create stirring sensual scenes that moved him to anticipate meeting her with an eagerness he hadn't felt in years.

Lily Andore. Obviously a pseudonym, but it conjured up pictures of a husky-voiced, sexy lady indeed, as did her writing. What would she be like?

As GABBY STALKED through the door to the kitchen, Mrs. James turned to glance over her shoulder and shook her head resignedly. "Were you baiting Mr. Graham again?" she accused.

"No, he was baiting me," Gabby declared firmly.

"Someone named Nina on the telephone," the housekeeper added, and at her words Gabby froze.

Nina! The blood receded, leaving her face almost colorless. Luckily Mrs. James was occupied at the counter opposite. Damn! She should have known that this would happen at the worst possible time. "Hello?"

"Gabby. I'm sorry to call you on your mother's telephone, but I have to see you." Nina's normally controlled voice was agitated.

"Where are you?" Her own voice was a thin quaver.

"I'm at a bistro on Columbus, across from the Museum of Natural History. You know, the one with the blue awning."

"I know it." It was across the street from the school at which she taught. "I'll be there in about five minutes," she said, and hung up.

It was the middle of March and winter still had a firm grip on New York City. Gabby walked down Seventy-seventh Street with her back to Central Park, shoulders hunched against the wind, hands buried in the pocket of her navy blue reefer, and her ponytail securely tucked up under a red wool toque.

Her mind was racing at a precarious speed. It had finally happened.

Nina waited for her at the door of the café, but not until they were seated at a small table in a corner did she meet Gabby's eyes. She tugged at the wiry gray curls that were so obviously premature. Not a line marred Nina's face except the two between her brows, and they were only the temporary result of worry. Finally she gave a resigned shrug.

Gabby relaxed in her chair with a sinking heart, knowing what was coming. "Well, Nina?" she asked.

"LILY ANDORE is *who*?" Henrietta dropped the telephone. She swung around to stare at her daughter as though she had suddenly found a snake in her parlor. Her hands fluttered to her face while the receiver dangled at the end of its cord, clattering noisily against the leg of the mahogany table.

Gabby winced for the poor ears of the person on the other end of the line. She tried to return the horrified gaze with a shrug and a smile, but when normally mild-mannered Henrietta looked at one like that it was difficult not to cringe.

Henrietta finally hoisted the receiver back, hand over hand, along the cord. She cleared her throat and said in a terse voice, "We'll *both* be waiting for you." Slamming down the phone, she fixed her daughter with an expression that had changed like lightning from dumbfounded to irate. "Would you care to explain, Gabriella?" she asked coldly.

Her mother, despite her very petite frame and ladylike manner, was a formidable woman when angered, no less so than Gabby herself. Much as she loved her, Gabby viewed the signs of Henrietta's temper with apprehension. The flushed cheeks, the intermittent flashes of silver from icy blue eyes, the narrow lips, all foretold a very unpleasant hour ahead. She knew because her own temper was as volatile as her mother's. It was perhaps the only characteristic they had in common.

The jig's up, thought Gabby irreverently and bit her lower lip, but she had known that since yesterday. The laugh that almost escaped wasn't prompted by amusement but rather by chagrin. She didn't feel really threatened—her mother loved her—but she did feel ten years old, and she lifted her chin just like the rebellious child she had once been. "You're the one who suggested I write a book!" she retorted defensively.

"A civilized book! A biography, a textbook! With your background in history.... But *this*! My God, I can't believe it!" Henrietta sank gracefully into a convenient chair and lifted slender fingers to her forehead in a dramatic gesture that was only partly contrived.

Gabby could well imagine that at this moment her mother fancied herself calling for her smelling salts like some tightly laced, overcome Victorian heroine. Except that there probably was no such thing as smelling salts today. In an age where admittedly weak, helpless women were almost extinct, her mother nevertheless occasionally mourned for a more gentle time. Her slight figure was structured on the framework of an iron will, but Henrietta did like drama and style. The role to be played today was obviously one of betrayal.

"This" referred to the historically accurate but

sizzling hot, sexy bestseller that was taking the country by storm. Gabby sighed. Obviously her mother knew now that Grabiella Constant was Lily Andore, notorious author of *Captive of Her Bed*.

Gabby watched her mother carefully. The next stage, after the anger and languishing despair, would be withdrawal; and the sooner her mother reached that "wash my hands of you" point, the better for Gabby. Henrietta would then retire to her room, leaving her daughter to mull over her words, or in this case try to figure out a way to hush things up.

But her escape was not to be so easy, not this time. Henrietta looked at her through her fingers. "I can't, I simply *can't* believe that *my* daughter wrote that book!"

It was Gabby's turn to be shocked. "Do you mean you've read it?" Her smoky gray eyes widened behind the outsize glasses. *Captive of Her Bed*, the story of Valentine Semmes, a nineteenth-century beauty who emerged from the slums of London to become one of the famous Parisian courtesans of the day, was not at all her mother's kind of thing.

Henrietta turned her eyes away as though she couldn't bear the strain. "I glanced through it. Hunter brought me a complimentary copy yesterday." Her head jerked around again as she remembered and her eyes widened in horror. "Hunter! He and Daphne are on their way over here right now!" She stood and began to pace the length of the room.

Gabby knew the answer, but she asked anyway rather timidly, "I suppose he's furious?"

"I think that would be a fair description of his mood," her mother stated. "He mentioned a radio talk show that aired in Boston."

Sinking deeper into the cushions of the sofa, Gabby groaned. She hadn't meant to say the things that had gone out over the air, but the interviewer had made her so mad!

"I never really thought the book would be published, you know," she offered with uncharacteristic meekness.

Henrietta ignored the apology. "I am going to make some tea," she said grandly. "I know the games you often play, Gabriella, and today you can simply handle it all yourself!"

With a half smile, Gabby watched her mother disappear into the hall. She wished she could disappear as easily to her own small apartment below. Why hadn't she made some kind of excuse when Henrietta had asked her earlier to come upstairs? She'd had her warning yesterday.

2

Having known for months that this moment was inevitable didn't make it any easier to face.

When the doorbell rang, Gabby was still alone in the living room. Apparently her mother had decided to leave her on her own to face Hunter and Daphne Cranston, his executive assistant. She caught a glimpse of herself in the mirror as she crossed the hall and, for the first time in her life, felt a twinge of regret for her looks.

She wore jeans and a sweat shirt and no makeup at all. Her dark hair was swept into its ever untidy ponytail. The heavy horn-rimmed glasses effectively hid her one outstanding feature, her eyes, which were a smoky, mysterious gray and heavily fringed with black lashes. Her lips were beautifully shaped but bloodless; and her skin, while smooth and unblemished, had a paleness that she thought made her look anemic. And who ever heard of an anemic Amazon?

She had inherited the pale coloring of her mother and the dark hair of her beautiful grandmother, and they didn't go together at all! She had also inherited the height from her father's side of the family. At five-foot-ten she towered over almost everyone she came in contact with. Long ago she had decided not to worry about her height. Her looks were hopeless anyway.

The bell rang again, more persistently this time. Gabby shrugged at her reflection and opened the door.

The two people who stood on the threshold stared at her with completely different expressions. One was curious, interested and held just the tiniest bit of amused sympathy. The other was a mixture of indignant wrath and transparent disgust.

Hunter Graham looked at the figure in scruffy jeans and huge sweat shirt, at the twist of unkempt hair and the pale face and gave a snort of disapproval. Damn! This... this tomboy could never have written *Captive of Her Bed*! He'd be willing to bet his company on it.

He leaned forward slightly at the waist for a closer look, searching for something, anything, to give lie to the thought. It would be impossible to define the figure inside those clothes. You couldn't even see her eyes behind the heavy glasses. The only concession he could make was that she had good cheekbones. His mouth twisted into a scornful grimace, and he wondered why he felt an odd sense of betrayal.

"*This* is Lily Andore?" he asked sarcastically.

The words sent the first color up to stain Gabby's cheeks, but she lifted her chin with a brave thrust and said evenly, "It's nice to see you, too. Won't you come in?"

He didn't even have the grace to look embarrassed, she thought angrily as she stepped back, allowing them to enter. "How are you, Daphne?" she inquired politely, taking their jackets.

Hunter's assistant was a close friend of her mother's and a frequent visitor to the house. Almost as tall as Gabby, she was the picture of the successful career woman. Her snapping brown eyes and smooth cinnamon-colored skin belied her age, for Gabby knew her to be in her late forties. Even dressed casually as she was today, in natural tweed slacks and a cranberry sweater, Daphne looked as though she had stepped right out of the pages of *Vogue*. When she spoke her voice was pleasingly low and calm. "I'm fine. How are you, Gabby?"

Gabby rolled her eyes instead of answering.

Daphne gave her a wink that called for patience and followed her employer into the living room.

As she hung their coats in the small closet off the hall, Gabby wondered what would happen if she simply walked out of the door behind her and disappeared forever. Her mother was playing Sarah Bernhardt and now Hunter seemed to be cast in the role of Dracula. All he needed was the cape and fangs. This was turning into a first-class farce!

"Where's your mother?" Hunter asked abruptly when she joined them.

Suddenly all of Gabby's earlier apprehension faded; it wasn't an inborn quality of hers anyway. She drew herself up to her full height. "Oh, was I mistaken?" she asked coolly. "I thought it was me you wanted to see, especially since you've gone to such trouble to discover my identity."

His eyes narrowed as though she'd insulted him. "Come off it, Gabby," he said sarcastically. "We all know you didn't write that book."

"What?" She returned the look with blank surprise.

Once more his eyes derisively raked the coltish figure before him. "Do you really expect me to believe you wrote *Captive* all by yourself? What do you know about lusty sex? Who helped you? Your mother? A *boy*friend?" He shook his head, his lips curving into a sneer as he accented the word the same way he'd done yesterday. "No. Your boyfriends probably don't have that much experience."

Rage boiled up in her until she felt she would explode. Her mouth gaping, she glared at him with murder in her eyes. Then she turned in silent appeal to Daphne, who came to her rescue.

"Why don't we sit down?" the older woman suggested calmly.

Hunter chose a wing-backed chair beside the fireplace as Daphne urged Gabby onto the sofa. "That's better," she said. "Now, can we discuss this situation like civilized adults?"

Gabby finally found her voice. "You and I can. I doubt that *he* knows the meaning of the word!" She shoved her glasses farther up on her nose with an irritated finger.

An unpleasant bark of laughter punctuated his speech. "Which one—'civilized' or 'adult'? Maybe when you grow up you'll learn the meaning of one of them yourself. You can bet that I never would have published that book if I'd known it was written by a child, no matter how precocious."

"I'm twenty-six years old!" she snapped back. "Hardly a child."

A deathly silence greeted her words. "One would never know it," Hunter finally declared, but his eyes were suddenly sharp. "Why do you let yourself look like that, then?" He gestured, indicating her appearance. It obviously offended him.

"Unfortunately, Mr. Graham, not all of us are born beautiful," she said defensively. There was an extraordinary lump in her throat at his offensive words and manner, but she refused to give in to the strange urge to cry. She knew the real reason he was angry. She had put one over on the Great Hunter Graham, and no one ever did that. "Besides, may I remind you that my book is making money for you. I shouldn't think that my lack of beauty would matter in that case."

"Beauty has nothing to do with it." He looked her over, a speculative gleam beginning in his eye. "I know a lot of fascinating women who are not beautiful, but they care enough about themselves to present a well-groomed appearance."

"I'm not interested in being beautiful or fascinating."

"That's obvious. If you really are twenty-six—"

"I am!" she interrupted.

"Then you could at least comb your hair! And your clothes are a mess! I'm supposed to send *this* on a national tour?" he finished with a lift of his brow.

His deep voice sent the censorious words over her with the force of an ocean wave, but she fought to keep from being caught in the undertow. "A national tour? I'm not going on a national tour," she protested flatly.

"Oh, yes, you are. Read your contract." He crossed his arms across his chest, made even more intimidatingly broad by the plaid shirt he wore. The strength of his long muscular legs was not disguised in his khaki slacks. He stretched them out in front of him and crossed his ankles.

"But I can't...!" Her palms began to sweat. Her head whirled. National tours, public appearances...

she hadn't counted on this. All those people...staring, prying; she just couldn't.

"Don't try to pretend you're a simple retiring schoolteacher, Gabby," he snapped. "It won't wash, because I've been on the receiving end of your sharp tongue."

"Of course I'm not retiring!" She pierced him with a glare that promptly withered under his own. This lecture was being delivered by a master, she conceded, but decided to give it one more try. She lifted her chin. "Or simple. You don't want to send me on tour," she added the obvious.

"Of course I don't." His eyes swept her up and down. "Look at you. I'll be laughed out of the business. Unfortunately the booksellers are demanding one, as well as the morning shows, the tabloids.... If *they* don't get what they want they'll make up whatever comes to mind." He eyed her speculatively. "On second thought that might be an improvement. No one could ever imagine Lily Andore to be an overgrown adolescent in a sweat shirt."

Daphne read Gabby's increasing agitation and put a comforting arm across her shoulder. "Graham, calm down," she scolded. "There's no need to be difficult."

"Difficult? I thought I was being very reasonable." Suddenly his demeanor showed a crack. "At least I'm not a devious, sneaky—"

"Graham!" Daphne would not be argued with this time.

Gabby hung her head miserably. This was worse, much worse, than she had imagined it would be. She had always been headstrong, but this time she had really jumped feet first into a mess.

What *was* in her contract? She had glanced through it when she signed, of course, but had not really understood the legalese. That was what an agent was for, after all, she thought with irritation. A memory made her pause. Yesterday Nina had tried to explain certain circumstances that might arise now that the book was a bestseller. She had waved them aside in the light of the information that Hunter was trying to reach her editor, out of town for the weekend, to discover the true identity of Lily Andore.

Never in her wildest imaginings would she have expected the degree of success that *Captive* had actually achieved. Nina had informed her that the book had sold more than eight thousand copies the first week and had already gone to a second printing.

A flash of inspiration lifted Gabby's head. "My job! I can't leave. I have a contract with the school, too."

Hunter got to his feet with an angry thrust. "Oh, hell!" He began to pace, his long stride covering the length of carpet in very few steps. He was visibly trying to calm himself, searching for a solution to an insolvable problem. At last he stopped short and looked down at her. "Tell me something, Gabby. Why did you write this book?" he asked.

"My mother has always wanted me to write," she told him, relaxing only slightly at the mild tone. Hunter seemed to have a hold on his temper, but she was still wary.

A dark brow lifted in disbelief and she went on to explain, "Mother is one of those people who think that if they can do something, anyone ought to be able to do it. Years ago she decided that I should write. We're very different, you see, but mother is always on the lookout for common ground." She gave a small smile at the thought of her mother, which Hunter met with a slight softening of his expression. Everyone who knew Henrietta loved her, even if she did frequently indulge her poetic temperament.

"What about your job? Are you unhappy teaching school?"

Gabby hesitated. "I'm...content," she answered slowly. "Not perfectly content, but satisfied for the time being." She knew that she wouldn't teach history to sixteen-year-old students for the rest of her life, but until she decided on an alternative, it was a job. "So, when mother kept harping and pushing me to try writing, I finally decided, why not?"

"But you didn't tell your mother."

It was not a question, but Gabby answered anyway. "No. Maybe I knew she wouldn't approve. I don't know. But I have my own apartment here, so I wrote at night."

"Your own apartment? I didn't know that." He frowned. "I thought you lived with your mother."

Gabby shook her head. "It's the ground-level flat downstairs. Mother fixed it up for me when I accepted the teaching job at a school nearby."

"Is, uh, is Henrietta afraid to let go of you?" He seemed embarrassed by his own question.

"Do you mean am I a mama's girl?" Gabby smiled slightly. "No. We each lead our own lives. It's simply more convenient like this."

"Okay, go on."

Gabby had filled eight legal pads of handwriting with what was the steamiest, sexiest historical love story to hit the shelves in years. She had taken it to a typist on the other side of town and given a false name. Finally, after a week or two of indecision, she'd mailed the whole manuscript to Graham House, using the school as a return address.

"Well," she continued aloud, "I had almost forgotten about the book." Hunter choked at this. "When the letter arrived from your office, I panicked. Then I thought of hiring an agent. I got Nina Worth out of the yellow pages."

Hunter had settled again in the chair facing her and listened to the recital without interruption, but he looked at his assistant when Daphne asked, "Why didn't you write something, ah, something...."

"Something tamer?" For the first time Gabby grinned sincerely. Maybe it was going to be all right after all. "I thought about it, but my whole life has been rather tame. I suppose I was ripe for something daring," she told them flippantly.

Hunter leaned forward in his chair, his hands dangling between his knees. "I should have known," he said, shaking his head. "And the revisions? I gave final approval and then turned the book over to the editor who'd recommended it, but I remember suggesting some changes."

"I did them all. I just never told the editor my real name. She knew I was a teacher and she had the number of my apartment. She could call after school hours if she needed to talk to me." Her eyes, behind their wall of glass, didn't reveal the degree of apprehension she had felt during the month that she'd worked on the revisions. What if her mother had dropped in during one of those lengthy conversations? "Anyway, when the book came out you were out of the country; I thought I was safe for a while."

"How did you get on the radio talk show?"

"Nina set that up with your office after last week's sales figures were in. They were urging me to do some publicity, but I didn't want to go on television," she said.

"I'm thankful for that at least," said Hunter, and Gabby bristled defensively.

"I do know my own limitations," she informed him. "And now, if the third degree is over...." She started to rise.

"It isn't," he said mildly. "*Captive of Her Bed* was completed ten months ago. Have you written anything since then?"

Unsteadily Gabby subsided against the sofa back. She was saved from answering when Henrietta entered the room. All three of them turned to look at her as though she were a creature from another century. Wearing a long floating gown, a wispy bit of chiffon pressed dramatically to her lips, she spread her weak smile among them. But Henrietta was stronger than she looked, as they all knew.

Gabby almost groaned aloud. Her mother was obviously going to play this drama to the final curtain.

Hunter recovered first. He rose politely and gave a helpless laugh as he looked at the dainty woman. "Come in, Henrietta. Don't worry. We won't bite."

"I heard you shouting, Hunter. You know I can't stand scenes." She drifted across the room, her bearing denying her pose of fragility. When she had arranged herself meticulously in a delicate French provincial chair she spoke again, still in that pale, shaded and totally fake voice. "Now, what about the radio show? What did, ah, Lily...say?"

Perfect timing, mother, thought Gabby, silently disgusted. *Absolutely perfect.* But much to her surprise, Hunter didn't erupt again.

He resumed his seat and propped his elbows on the arms of his chair. Building a tower with his fingers, he looked over them at Gabby, but it was to her mother that he spoke. "Do you know what yesterday was, Henrietta?" he asked in response to her question.

Gabby was sure she was mistaken when she thought she saw a gleam of laughter in his eyes.

Her mother looked from one to the other of them blankly. "Saturday?"

"Saturday, the seventeenth of March, and Saint Patrick's Day. Yesterday morning our author told the predominantly Celtic population of Boston that St. Patrick was really an Englishman and the holiday was just an excuse to drink green beer and party all night. Besides, she added, when did an Irishman ever need an excuse to do that? She informed her interviewer that 'banned in Boston' was a silly expression, considering all the corruption in Massachusetts politics. Bostonians were nothing but a bunch of hypocrites."

Silence greeted his words. Henrietta turned slowly to stare at her daughter.

"Well," Gabby said defensively, "he was saying that my book would never have made it to the bookstores in that city fifty years ago."

"And the Irishmen?" Her mother's question was only a whisper.

"The interviewer was obnoxious. He kept trying

to tell me that my hero should have been Irish, because they are the only real men left." She glanced down at her hands clenched in her lap and then up again to meet Hunter's eyes. "He'd been into the poteen quite heavily, I suspect."

"I understand that the station's lines were jammed until well after midnight with people crying for your blood. Boston will be the first stop on your tour, I think," he mused.

"That would solve your problem nicely," snapped Gabby. "It would save you the trouble of wringing my neck. But, as I told you, I'm not going on tour."

"And as I told you—read your contract!" Hunter responded. "Or didn't your agent explain the finer points to you?"

"But my job..." Gabby reminded him.

Hunter raked through the black hair with an impatient hand, but he seemed to have kept the firm hold on his temper when he spoke again. "How are we going to work this out? Can you get some time off?" he asked.

"No," Gabby said in a voice that told him clearly he'd have an argument on his hands if he tried to force the issue. "You don't take time off during the school year if you're a teacher."

"Look here, Gabby—" he began irritably.

Once again Daphne's good sense intruded into a conversation that promised to renew his antagonism. "Maybe we *can* arrange something. Gabby, could you manage weekends for the time being?"

"That's an idea," Hunter put in, giving his assistant an approving glance.

Gabby held her tongue for once, giving herself a minute to think. She didn't want to do this, she really didn't. "Look, Hunter. I'm not the type to go all over the country signing autographs. You've found out how well my interviews go. I'd just end up making everyone mad."

"But you would sell books," Hunter observed. "The Boston bookstores are begging for you. They say the crowds will come if you're there, even if it's only to get a look at the enemy."

He was pleased, she realized in stunned amazement. He didn't care what she said if it sold books. He hadn't been angry because of her remarks; he had been angry because she'd hoodwinked the Great Hunter Graham.

"Like this?" She indicated her attire in another plea for understanding.

Hunter was not to be swayed. "You're right." He rose and walked slowly across to look down at her where she sat on the sofa. His size was overpowering, and she had to make an effort not to shrink back into the cushions. Casually he rested his hands on his lean hips and did a thorough, leisurely inventory, from the toes of her sneaker-clad feet to the untidy ponytail. It took forever.

How strange, thought Gabby. *I've watched him inspect other women with the same intensity and wondered at the effect on them. Now I know.*

Her heartbeat seemed to speed up, at the same time becoming erratic, sending her heated blood on a wild pulsating ride through her veins. She was helplessly aware of the involuntary changes in her body. Her nipples hardened, her breasts swelled, until her bra felt uncomfortable and binding. A heaviness in the lower regions of her body was both exciting and frightening. God, he was potent! Was he aware of what he was doing to her? Of course he was, a man of his experience. One corner of his mouth twitched. *Let me go*, she cried inside.

His attention swung to his assistant, and she could finally breathe again. The incident had lasted only seconds, but Gabby felt that she had aged dramatically.

"Daphne, make an appointment with one of those salons over on Park Avenue. I don't care what we spend, but we certainly can't send her out looking like this." His eyes returned to hold Gabby's gaze. "Arrange it right away. Fix her up," he said as though she were a piece of furniture badly in need of repair.

At the dispiriting words a semblance of rationality replaced her dazed awe, giving her the strength for a protest of sorts. "What if I don't want to be 'fixed up'?" she asked, hoping he couldn't hear the unsteadiness in her voice.

He leaned forward to plant a hand on either side of her head. There was a subduing gleam in his eyes. His fresh breath fanned the sensitive skin of her face. "Then you'll just have to learn to bear it, little girl," he said in a low, determined voice.

3

"Do you have a spring vacation coming up, Gabby?" Daphne was all business as she spoke into the silence that followed Hunter's departure.

"Yes," Gabby admitted reluctantly. "Next week."

"Wonderful! That will give us time to really get going." She reached into her purse for the appointment book she always carried. "What are the dates?"

"I've never been to a beauty salon before," Gabby announced, avoiding the answer.

Daphne just managed to keep her jaw from dropping. "Who cuts your hair?" she asked bluntly. "No, never mind." She shook her head. "Just give me the dates."

With a resigned sigh Gabby gave them to her. "But, Daphne, I really don't want to go on a tour."

Daphne patted her hand. "I know, dear, but it's been decreed. Just enjoy it," she suggested pleasantly.

"Enjoy it? How can I possibly enjoy it? I hate crowds! And the only people I'm accustomed to addressing are sixteen-year-old history students. What will I say?"

"The same things you said on the radio," Daphne answered calmly. Before Gabby's horrified gasp could leave her lips the older woman went on, "Maybe you shouldn't be quite as candid as you were to the Boston audience, but it did stir up interest."

"But that was on the radio," Gabby protested.

"What difference does it make?" Daphne asked, genuinely puzzled.

Bless Daphne, she just didn't understand. Gabby got to her feet. Her sneakers began to trace the same path that Hunter's Gucci loafers had trod a short while ago. How could she answer? Her looks had never mattered much to her at all, so how could she say now that she was self-conscious? Brought up in a family of dainty, tiny women, she had never even tried to compete, choosing instead to be herself. She was intelligent, educated, healthy and well adjusted. Why should she try to be glamorous, too, when glamour was not her style? She did feel a twinge of regret, however, for the way she looked today.

That memory triggered another: Hunter's derisive inventory when he had entered the room and his assumption at first that she wasn't capable of writing the book. Her anger swelled again. Damn him, he had shown himself to be everything she most despised in a man—autocratic, pompous and with an ego second to none. Though he'd calmed down afterward she found that she would still love to teach him a lesson about jumping to conclusions. He thought he could come in here and dictate to her, did he? Could she make him eat his words?

Shoving her hands into the pockets of her jeans, she turned to face the two women who watched her. "Daphne, I don't know what you think can be done, but you're welcome to try. I suppose I have no choice anyway."

"No, dear, you haven't. But let me reassure you about Hunter. He's not always that overbearing. It's just that you took him by surprise, and Hunter is not used to surprises."

Gabby gave a sniff. "I'm sure I don't care what his attitude is toward me."

Daphne looked skeptical. "Well, I just want you to know that his bark is worse than his bite."

Henrietta laughed. Both pairs of eyes swung to her. "Gabby's isn't," she said.

It was the first sound she'd made since her entrance.

"Isn't what?" Daphne asked with a blank stare.

"Worse than her bite. She takes after me, I'm afraid," Henrietta admitted with a faint smile. "I have a shocking temper. I'm not so sure that I don't feel just a little bit sorry for Hunter." She chuckled. Gone was the delicate heroine. Gabby noted with satisfaction that the drama was over. The curtain had rung down on act three, and her mother was once again herself.

"Mother! How can you say that?" Gabby tried to glare at her mother, but her relief was too obvious. When their eyes met, the two women simultaneously dissolved into laughter.

"I'm sorry that I overreacted, dear," her mother apologized when she could speak again.

"That's okay, mother. I understand," Gabby said graciously. "It was too good an opportunity to miss, wasn't it? After all, it isn't every day you have the chance to play an outraged parent."

Her mother dimpled. "I did get rather carried away, didn't I?" She plucked at the chiffon skirt.

"Mother, the Divine Sarah couldn't have done it better," Gabby proclaimed.

"Thank you, dear," Henrietta said primly. After a pause she went on, "You really wrote that book?"

"Yes, mother."

"You're going to make a lot of money, aren't you." Was that a trace of envy in her statement?

Gabby grinned. "Yes, I think so."

Daphne looked from one to the other of them. "Definitely!" she said. "I thought I knew you two well, but I didn't realize that either of you had bad tempers."

"Oh, neither of us stays mad very long," Gabby promised. "But we are definitely touchy."

When Gabby finally closed the door of her apartment downstairs she breathed a long sigh and headed for her tiny but well-equipped kitchen to pour herself a glass of wine. She very seldom drank anything, even under the pressure of being with rowdy teenagers every day, but tonight she needed something to relax her.

Was the worst over, she asked herself as she wandered back into her small living room. She selected an album of Brahms and put it on the stereo before sinking gratefully into a wicker rocking chair. Her first taste of the crisp dry wine was an eager swallow rather than a sip, and she almost choked. She set the glass on a small table and rested her head against the puffy cushion, allowing her eyes to roam the room.

Her apartment was her own haven. She'd done the walls in white to create an airy atmosphere. Grandmother's wicker was also white and comfortably padded with intensely colored striped and flowered cushions. Rather than have heavy draperies like those upstairs she'd chosen louvered shutters to cover the windows. Her haven—but would it be enough when the intrusions began?

Those intrusions were something that she had dreaded since the day a little more than a year ago when she'd received the letter accepting her manuscript. There wasn't a bashful bone in her body, she knew that, but with strangers...could she cope? Inside her there had always been a small part that was private, that she shielded from the world.

The telephone rang, interrupting her reverie.

"May I come over for a while this evening, Gabby?" Steven asked.

She hesitated. She was tired, drained. Still, Steven wasn't a demanding person to entertain and it probably would be a good time to tell him about Lily. "Yes, Steven, that will be fine. Come about seven and I'll make us an omelet."

While waiting for him Gabby took a shower and dressed in a fresh pair of jeans and a bulky sweater. She brushed her hair back into its ponytail, where it stayed neatly for about five minutes before the springy fullness began to fight free.

"You're looking lovely this evening, Gabby," said Steven without sparing her a glance.

And that is a meaningless platitude if I ever heard one, thought Gabby. For a fleeting second she suspected that she liked Hunter's honest insults better. She stood aside to let Steven enter. Her eyes, behind the thick glasses, contemplated him. Steven was her own height and bone thin where Hunter was sinewy and strong. Steven's shoulders had a tendency to slope, but Hunter's shoulders were.... What on earth was she doing? Gabby shifted her thoughts away from any further comparisons. They weren't fair to Steven, who was really a very nice person, much nicer than....

"Would you like a glass of wine, Steven?" she asked as she led the way into the kitchen.

"Thank you." Steven hitched his gray trousers and sat neatly on one of the ladder-backed chairs at her kitchen table. She had already set out placemats and silver. Plates were warming in the oven and preparations for supper were under way.

Gabby poured Steven's wine and topped off her own, her second glass. She joined him at the table. Might as well get it over with. "Steven, I have a confession to make."

He smiled at her. "This sounds serious."

With her chin propped on her hand she smiled back. "It is." She took a breath. "I am Lily Andore."

"Who?" He looked blank.

She laughed. "Thank you, Steven." He was a dear, she decided. "I have written a novel, and I used the pen name of Lily Andore," she explained carefully. "It seems to be doing very well."

"Oh? Well, you know, Gabby, that I seldom read novels."

"Steven," she said gently, "it's number one on the *New York Times* list this week."

"And *never* bestsellers," he said, horrified.

She had to hold her sides to keep from splitting.

THE STUDENTS were restless all week. Spring holidays would start with the weekend. A number of them were planning trips to the east coast of Florida to join the annual influx of "snowbirds" from Daytona Beach south to Fort Lauderdale.

Gabby envied them. How wonderful it would be to look forward to a week spent lazing in the sun, instead of the week of heaven-knows-what that *she* would have to endure. As Friday drew near her nervousness increased.

Daphne called every day offering encouragement. Her motives were comically obvious. The pep talks didn't really help, though, and Gabby faced the Saturday-morning appointment at the makeover salon with growing apprehension.

Henrietta was no help at all. She wasn't quite sure what her attitude should be this time—protective toward her only child, as she had always been, or supportive of the changes that she had seen the need for but never insisted on. She fluttered around Gabby's apartment all week, never finishing a sentence, unable to sit still for more than a few minutes, until finally Gabby sent her upstairs to her office with instructions to balance her checkbook. That job always took her mother several days.

Gabby had enough to do, grading finals and averaging them for the students' report cards. When Friday finally arrived the hectic pace of the week had taken its toll. She had an early dinner and went to bed to fall immediately into a deep sleep.

Saturday dawned bright, clear and cold. Gabby dressed in her favorite outfit, a navy blue wool pants suit with a comfortable boxy jacket. Underneath it she wore a gray sweater. Her hair was swept neatly into its ever present ponytail. She really thought she looked quite presentable until she walked with

Daphne into one of the exclusive salons of beauty on Park Avenue.

They were shown at once to a private room where waited two of the most awesome individuals Gabby had ever seen in her life. A feeling of total inadequacy overcame her despite the fact that she towered over both of them.

The man was presented to her as Monsieur Jacques and the woman as Madame Marie. They were dark elfin creatures, the man only slightly taller than the woman. Gabby hoped they spoke English; her college French was more than rusty—it was nonexistent.

The two bowed stiffly and proceeded to take her apart with their eyes, piece by piece, all the time clucking and shaking their heads sadly.

Monsieur Jacques indicated with a wave of his hand that Gabby should revolve. When her back was turned he reached up, without warning, and painfully swept off the rubber band that held her hair.

"Ouch! That—" Gabby bit back the rest of her protest as she whirled on him.

The thick dark mane spilling down her back had provoked the first glimmer of interest. He was fingering the texture of her hair as if it were a piece of fabric he wanted to identify. With an extravagantly flamboyant gesture he threw the band into the corner and exclaimed, "Never again put your hair up like that! The band breaks the fragile strands and leaves your hair looking like you stuck your finger in a light socket!"

He spoke English all right, thought Gabby, and with barely a whit of an accent, but it appeared that these two would be even more domineering than

Hunter. She looked helplessly at Daphne, who returned her look with one of pity and addressed the man. "Do you know what has to be done?"

"*Oui*. Hunter Graham called me personally!" he said grandly, pointing to his chest. "He said that it was a *very* important job."

"Then I shall leave you to it," Daphne told him. "See you later, Gabby."

"Daphne! You're not leaving?" Gabby said in a horrified voice. "Please stay!"

"I'd be in the way, dear. Don't worry; they won't turn you into a monster."

Gabby wasn't so sure, however, as she was examined, poked and prodded. There were glances exchanged, unrecognizable mutterings and many Gallic shrugs and gestures. Finally Madame Marie pulled the jacket from her shoulders and Gabby received a definite nod of approval. "Nice figure," said the woman casually. Her accent was much stronger—it came out "nize feegure."

"Excellent," agreed the man. He rested his elbow in one palm and stroked his chin speculatively with the fingers of his other hand.

An irreverent memory surfaced of a mad scientist in an old movie she'd once seen. All Monsieur Jacques needed was a waxed goatee. Gabby bit her lip to keep from smiling. This was obviously very serious business indeed, and she had a feeling that a smile would not be welcome.

"We'll have to see the legs, though," he went on matter-of-factly. Then he must have caught the expression of dismay on Gabby's face.

Suddenly his eyes warmed with a friendly smile. His stiff reserve and that of his co-worker melted away. "Please, don't pay any attention to us," he apologized. "Sometimes we tend to speak around our clients rather than to them."

"Certainly, uh, *monsieur*. I understand."

"Call us Jacques and Marie," he offered. "Since we will be working together for several days—"

"Days! But I thought...."

Jacques ignored her interruption. "You won't mind if we dispense with the formality?"

"Of course not," said Gabby. "I'm delighted." She smiled feebly. "Do you know how intimidating you two are? You scared me to death when I first came in."

He laughed. "Naturally. It's the image we cultivate for most of our customers, who need to be bullied into doing what they should. But you...Mr. Graham suggested that encouragement and a little boost to your self-confidence would work better."

"He did?" asked Gabby in a weak voice. She was surprised and strangely warmed by the revelation.

The small man nodded. "Was he right?"

"I—I don't know," she answered with complete honesty. "I've never done this before."

"Well, we shall see," said Marie. "We would not hesitate to revert to bullying you if it were necessary."

They went back to their study of her eyes, her facial structure, her hair, her figure. Marie made notes; Jacques thumbed through a huge leather-bound book filled with pictures and color swatches. They consulted about pH balance, toners and rinses, hot-oil treatments (she was really suspicious of that!) and alkalines and acids versus neutralizers. It sounded like a chemistry class.

Finally Gabby was led away to undress and don a smock provided by Marie. "We will not be able to do more than get started today," she told Gabby, her accent heavier when seasoned with enthusiasm. "By the end of next week you will not know yourself."

Gabby supposed that Marie meant to be reassuring, and she tried to respond with the same eagerness. "Wonderful!" she said, effectively disguising the dismay in her voice.

When she left the Park Avenue salon late that afternoon, her hair had been trimmed to sweep below her shoulders in the back and feather around her jaw in front. It moved when she walked, she discovered, and the feeling was rather nice. Jacques had threatened to shave her head if he ever caught her using the rubber band again.

Marie had given her the first manicure.

"The first? Will I need another one?" Gabby had asked, looking up in surprise from the shaped ovals of her nails. They were clear of polish but buffed to a high shine.

"Every day," Marie had informed her. "You must put this cream on your hands at night and sleep in these white cotton gloves."

"Yuck! It's greasy," Gabby had complained, testing the cream between her thumb and forefinger.

"That's why you wear the gloves," the other woman had explained patiently. "And every time you put your hands in water, you must use this lotion." She'd handed Gabby another bottle and then another. "This is for your face at night. We'll start on makeup next week."

Finally the formidable pair had waved her out.

"Be here Monday morning at nine," Jacques had ordered.

She arrived at the brownstone to find her mother having a glass of sherry with Hunter Graham. When she tried to sneak back out to go to her own apartment, Henrietta called to her.

"Come here, dear. We want to see what you look like." As Gabby came forward, Henrietta's face fell in disappointment. "Your hair is pretty," she said weakly.

Gabby laughed for the first time since her morning's ordeal had begun and risked a glance in Hunter's direction. "This is only the beginning, mother. They can't undo a lifetime of bad habits in one day." All the same she was deflated when Hunter made no comment on her hair. She thought it looked rather nice. Excusing herself, she started to leave the room, but was brought up short by his low vibrant voice.

"I'll be over tomorrow with Daphne, Gabby. Please leave the afternoon free."

She turned back to him. "Whatever for?"

As his eyes drifted over her well-disguised shape, Gabby felt the most ridiculous urge to slide the boxy jacket from her shoulders. Marie had said she had a good figure and just once she'd like to get a positive reaction from this man. Except that it might not *be* positive. The Great Hunter Graham was well known for escorting beautiful women, and a passable figure was certainly nothing new for him. Besides, she still wasn't a blonde.

When he spoke there was a derisive gleam in his eye. "To coach you for further interviews, of course. We don't want any more debacles like the one that occurred in Boston, do we?"

"We don't?" she asked sweetly. "I thought you were pleased with that. It sold books."

"Yes, it sold books, which incidentally makes a lot of money for you, too," he countered bluntly. "So do you think you could be cooperative for once in your life, instead of balking at everything we're trying to do for you?"

The question made her really angry. She wasn't sure why. Maybe it was because of that condescension in his attitude again, maybe because he hadn't complimented her on her hair. Her anger might even be irrational, but she couldn't put it down. She rolled her eyes heavenward. "I'm supposed to be *grateful* when you bully me?" she shouted.

"I'm not bullying you!" he roared. "I'm just making an effort to polish you up a bit."

The meaning of the term "speechless with fury" had always escaped her until this moment, but she couldn't have spoken had her life depended on it. She turned on her heel and stalked from the room.

THE NEXT AFTERNOON was a disaster. Even with Daphne there to referee, Gabby and Hunter still could barely be civil.

"How can I know what I'll say when I don't know what the questions will be?" she ranted at the end of an hour.

"Well, there's one thing you'd damn well better practice, and that's how to control that childish temper!" he snarled.

Daphne finally managed to shepherd him out the door, with a promise to keep working with Gabby until she was perfect.

Gabby stamped her foot. "That is the most *mad-*

dening man, Daphne. How do you stand working for him?''

Daphne didn't ever answer directly, but murmured something that served. In fact she had worked for Hunter Graham for ten years and his father before him, and she had never seen him act like this, especially to an author who was making tons of money for him.

ON THURSDAY MORNING when Gabby entered the salon she was greeted by an excited Jacques with the announcement that Mr. Graham himself would be by after lunch to see the results of her makeover and take her shopping.

''Take me shopping? *He's* going to take me shopping? Over my dead body,'' she declared hotly.

Jacques and Marie practically had to tie her down to get her new contact lenses into her eyes and her makeup applied. When Jacques finally removed the last heated roller from her hair, she was still protesting. ''Bend over,'' he ordered, brandishing the hairbrush.

''You wouldn't!'' Gabby's voice dropped to a shocked whisper.

He erupted with a bark of laughter. ''Don't tempt me. I meant your head.''

''Oh.'' Gabby obligingly bent her head forward between her knees while Jacques brushed vigorously.

''Now, sling it back.''

Gabby complied. Her hair flew back and settled into a dark cloud around her face. A few touches with the brush and he stepped back to view his work. Marie came up beside him and they both stood for a moment looking at her. Marie cocked her head to one side and Jacques frowned.

Gabby's heart plummeted to her toes. "It didn't work, did it?" she asked in a small voice.

They were both startled by her question. "What?" they chorused.

"You've done your best, I know, and I love you both for trying, but I'm still me, aren't I?"

Marie came forward quickly to envelop her in a warm hug. Then Jacques threw his arms around them both. "Gabby, you're beautiful! Can't you see for yourself?"

"But I haven't changed! I thought I would be different!" she wailed.

"Of course not. Our job wasn't to make you something that you're not," he explained patiently. "We simply embellished what you already had."

"Like improving the lighting on a fine painting," Marie added. "It was all there to begin with, but you couldn't see it properly."

Slowly Gabby turned to face the mirror again. She leaned forward to examine the delicate blush of coloring on her smooth skin, the subtle lighter streaks in her hair that seemed to give the rich dark thickness a lift, a vitality of its own. The unruly brows were now shaped in perfect arches to frame her smoky eyes dramatically. Her thick lush lashes still didn't need mascara, but they were no longer hidden by the heavy horn-rimmed lenses. Her pale lips glistened with a glossy peach stain.

She straightened to her full height and squared her shoulders, tilting her chin slightly upward as she had been taught. Even in the shapeless smock she could see the improvement. "Do you mean I could have looked like this all along?'' she breathed. All the years of envying her mother's petite blonde beauty, all the years.... She shook her head ruefully.

Marie took a breath. "Now, Gabby, I am going to turn back into Madame Marie for a minute," she warned, planting her hands on her hips.

Gabby grinned. "You mean that intimidating person I met on the first day?"

"Right. I want you to pay attention to me. Mr. Graham is taking you to Betsy Powers's boutique this afternoon."

Stiffening at the mention of his name, Gabby tried to protest, but Marie wasn't listening.

"I have talked to Betsy at length and she has a number of things for you to try on, things that were selected especially to complement your coloring and your figure. All the makeup and hairstyling we have done will be even more effective if you dress in becoming clothes."

Jacques added his piece, shaking a finger into Gabby's startled face. "Don't you *ever* let me catch you in navy blue again!" He shuddered. "When I think of that suit you wore in here.... You looked positively yellow!"

Marie nodded her agreement. "Betsy is preparing a color chart for you to use in the future when you purchase clothes, but for now I want you to be guided by her."

"And those glasses—" Jacques winced. "Throw them away! You must always wear your contact lenses to let the world see your wonderful eyes!"

For a few moments Gabby didn't answer, but finally she shrugged. "Okay."

They had obviously been prepared for an argument, because they both visibly relaxed at the word.

TWO HOURS LATER she stood stark naked in the middle of a room made endless by mirrors. Her arms shielded her body in a vague attempt at modesty as the chic woman in her fifties handed her a scrap of lace to replace her panties. "If you wish to look beautiful, you must *feel* beautiful from the skin out. Where *did* you get that bra? Inherit it from your grandmother?"

"My lingerie is none of your concern!" Gabby tried for assurance in her voice as she hopped on one leg to scramble into the bikini panties, but it was a hopeless effort in the face of such determination.

"*That*, my dear—" the woman shuddered "—could never be called lingerie. *That* is underwear!"

Gabby blushed. "Nevertheless, I am here for clothes, not all...all this," she said, indicating the mountain of lace and satin, silk and illusion, piled on every surface.

"Nevertheless," Betsy Powers mocked her, "this comes first."

There was no arguing with the woman. With a grouchy sigh, Gabby gave in, allowing herself to be fitted with bras in every style and color, teddies, panties, slips and petticoats of glorious silken fabrics and lace so delicate it was like a cobweb.

Finally Mrs. Powers gave a nod of approval and called one assistant to take away half of the mountain and a second to bring in the first creation.

No, it could never be called a dress. It was a fairy-tale fantasy of creamy white georgette embroidered from neck to hem with tiny seed pearls and bright silvery beads. It fit perfectly, clinging to her shape like a lover. The last were Mrs. Powers's words and Gabby had to admit that they were apropos. When she faced herself she caught her breath. In this sleek column of a gown she looked totally female and quite striking. "I guess the right clothes do work wonders," she admitted on a breath.

"Exactly," agreed Mrs. Powers. "So now, my dear, will you please let me do my job without any further interference?"

"Yes, ma'am," Gabby agreed meekly.

"Good. Come along." Mrs. Powers opened the door to the hall.

"Where are we going?" Gabby gingerly lifted the slim skirt and started to follow.

"Hunter wants to see you."

At that she stopped. "No," she said in a cross voice. She wasn't ready to face him yet. The drive to the boutique had passed in total silence. The grim-faced man had barely taken one quick look at her when he picked her up at the salon, thanked Jacques and Marie shortly and hustled her into the back of a cab without a single word about her appearance.

Gabby had bitten her lip to keep from giving him the satisfaction of asking what he thought.

Mrs. Powers either didn't hear or preferred to ignore her negative response. She disappeared through the door leading to the showroom, and Gabby had no choice but to follow.

Their heads were together. They were speaking in low tones. Suddenly Hunter lifted his eyes to meet Gabby's and he broke off in midsentence. Slowly his gaze slid down the full length of her, taking in every detail, and then traveled back up at the same languorous speed.

Gabby had the feeling that he knew how each tiny bead and pearl was attached by the time he met her eyes again. Still he didn't offer a compliment. Damn him! She wanted to stomp her foot in chagrin... until she noticed something.

The Great Hunter Graham was holding his breath.

For the first time in her life Gabby felt the power of her femininity as it grew and flowered under his gaze. Of course, she was not entirely without experience of the opposite sex. She had dated since her teens. On a whim she had even become engaged to an artist when she was in college, though the engagement hadn't lasted more than a few days. But those had been boys. Never had she seen the expression on a man's face that Hunter now wore.

His eyes were slightly glazed, she noted with growing delight. The black pupils opened to merge with the dark brown circles around them, widening involuntarily, as though to take in as much of the sight of her as possible. His lips parted slightly to let out his breath in a soundless stream.

Gleeful exhilaration surged through Gabby. She took a step and turned. "Do you like it?" she asked playfully over her shoulder, holding her arms slightly away from her body as she had been taught.

He pressed his lips together, biting off what would have been his first, honest reaction, and the dimple in his cheek deepened. "Very nice." He seemed to choke slightly on the words.

But Gabby had seen what he would have hidden, and she was satisfied for now.

The next dress was a drama in black. It was of thin silk damask with soft pouf sleeves and ruffles that raced down the plunging neckline almost to her waist. The full floor-length skirt barely wrapped around her, showing a generous glimpse of calf and knee when she walked. When she reappeared in the showroom, Hunter seemed to have recovered somewhat from the first shock, but his eyes did linger on the shadowy hollow between her breasts for rather a long time. Gabby almost laughed aloud. This was fun, she told herself happily.

There was a peach-colored lace halter top with a copper satin skirt and cummerbund. There were day dresses in lawn and tissue silk, suits in the softest cashmere and weightless wool crepe. There were blouses and skirts, shoes and sweaters; there were slacks and cropped little tops, and there was even a pair of jeans—not her old faithful Levi's but a pair that clung to her rounded derriere like a second skin and had somebody's name on the back pocket. The colors were a heavenly garden—lemon and fuchsia, deep rose and heather, robin's egg blue and moss green.

She didn't model everything for Hunter, but whenever she did appear, the gleam in his eyes that sparkled in response to her smile was enough of a reward. She began to anticipate the warmth that sang through her body when his gaze lingered. This exciting feeling was heady, exhilarating.

It was nearing five-thirty when Hunter suggested they call it a day. "Betsy's probably ready to close up shop."

Mrs. Powers didn't demur, but she looked very satisfied and pleased with herself as she smiled benignly at Gabby.

And well she should, thought Gabby. *I've just spent the next six months' allowance from grandmother's trust fund.* "I'll go and change." She was wearing a crepe de chine tunic in a soft amethyst color and matching slim pants.

"Why don't you leave that on?" Hunter suggested. "I'll take you somewhere for dinner."

Strappy silver sandals brought her height to six feet, but even so she had to look up to Hunter when he rose. "Really?" Was that Gabby Constant who sounded so thrilled? For a brief moment a cloud shadowed her eyes. Or was it Lily Andore? She dismissed any misgivings. Whoever it was, she was having a wonderful time.

Hunter put out a finger to brush her cheek, sending a rush of deeper color to her hairline. "Really," he said with casual amusement. His hand lingered on her shoulder and the amusement died in his eyes, to be supplanted by an unexpected flash of desire. His fingers tightened, bringing her closer until there was barely an inch between them.

Gabby felt the same hot rushing in her veins that she'd experienced in her mother's parlor that day—less than two weeks ago?—when Hunter had looked at her for the first time as a woman. But then he'd been disappointed by what he saw, and today he was pleased.

He didn't seem to be able to detach his gaze from her dark smoky eyes. "Betsy, didn't I see a wrap of some kind?" he said huskily.

"Yes. I'll get it." Neither of them noticed when the woman left the showroom.

Hunter's brilliant stare dropped to her lips. Slowly he bent his head until their mouths brushed. His other hand came up to slide carefully around her waist, drawing her lightly against the lower part of his body.

Gabby closed her eyes and sighed. He caught the sound with a deeper kiss, his mouth opening over hers, warm and moist and tender, but still lightly, as though he were afraid to let himself go for fear of frightening her.

She breathed his name, earning herself a deep hoarse chuckle before he put her reluctantly away from him.

Her lids felt as heavy as lead, but she forced them open to meet his gentle smile with a dazed one of her own.

"Betsy's coming," he warned in a whisper, a moment before the woman came bustling into the room.

"Here we are." She had a long black velvet evening cloak over her arm.

Hunter reached in his pocket to withdraw a slip of paper, which he handed to Mrs. Powers. "Put it all on my bill and have everything delivered to this address."

Gabby came down to earth fast. "Wait just a minute. What are you talking about?"

He chuckled. "I'm talking about all these feathers for you to fly with."

"You're not buying my clothes," she stated flatly.

He frowned. "Don't be silly, Gabby. I forced you into this. Of course I'll pay for it."

Her chin came up defiantly. "You will not," she told him heatedly. "I don't need your charity."

Mrs. Powers tried to help but made matters much worse instead. "Hunter does this, uh, he's been...."

At Hunter's furious glare the poor woman swallowed and murmured, "Excuse me." She disappeared in a hurry.

Gabby felt a wave of embarrassment. He had done this before. He had watched other women as they preened in front of him just as she had done. The thought took the glow out of her eyes. "I'm sure you are used to buying clothes for all your women friends, inamoratas or whatever, but I am none of those and I buy my own clothes!"

He put a hand on her arm. "Look, honey—"

She slapped it away. "I am *not* your honey!"

"Gabby, calm down. These things are for the tour!" he growled.

"Oh? And do I give them back when the tour is over?" she asked with a mutinous tilt of her head.

"Of course not," he said impatiently.

"Then I'll pay."

He took her arm again, this time with a grip that refused to be dislodged, and grabbed up his coat and the velvet cloak. "We'll argue about it over dinner."

4

AND ARGUE THEY DID, from cocktails throughout the delicious meal.

"You can't pay for all this on a teacher's salary, and you won't get a royalty check until July. Be reasonable," Hunter urged.

Gabby took a sip of wine to cool her throat. "I have a trust fund from my grandmother's estate," she told him. "I'll consider it an investment in myself."

Hunter grudgingly gave in over dessert when he realized that she wasn't to be budged. He still insisted on paying for the makeover, however, and Gabby finally conceded on that point.

"You are a stubborn woman," he grated. "Would you like to dance?" His words were delivered in a voice strangely and abruptly different.

Gabby blinked. Woman? Not girl? "Yes," she answered.

Hunter led her to the dance floor, one hand holding hers in a tight grip as he practically dragged her along in his wake. *He must really be upset to forget good manners so completely*, Gabby was thinking, but then he turned her into his arms and suddenly all rational thought was gone.

The sensation of being held by such a tall man was one of heart-expanding luxury. Immediately Gabby relaxed in a glow of contentment.

Hunter's arm encircled her back completely, cradling her against him until they fit together like hand and glove. His warm breath stirred the hair at her temple and the scent of his cologne added to the enchantment. She felt light on her feet, airy, as she followed his steps in perfect rhythm. Smoothly they moved together to the romantic ballad for a few minutes, his hand on the curve of her waist provoking all sorts of wanton responses.

Hunter pulled back slightly to look down at her with a tender smile that went to her heart like an arrow. "This is the quietest you've been all night. What are you thinking?" His soft murmur washed over her, leaving her even weaker, more disoriented.

When she answered her voice was unconsciously beguiling. "I was thinking how nice it is to dance with a really tall man."

"We do fit together nicely, don't we?" he answered in equally seductive tones.

She nodded and his arm tightened, bringing her back against him. "I don't dance much," she admitted. "It isn't easy to follow a partner if you're looking down at the top of his head."

"How do you think I feel when my date's nose is in my belt buckle?" He chuckled.

She looked up with a surprised laugh. "I never thought about that. I suppose you feel stiff and uncomfortable, too. Sorority dances used to be a nightmare until...." Her voice trailed off. Those memories brought back the old Gabby, and tonight she was Lily Andore. She was Sleeping Beauty and Cinderella, and she refused to think about the rumpled history teacher of a week ago.

"Until what?" he prodded.

The gleam in her eyes was teasing. "Until I discovered the basketball team."

He threw back his head with a laugh of pure enjoyment. "That sounds more like Lily Andore than Gabby Constant," he taunted.

"Tonight I feel a little bit like her," she admitted unguardedly, surprised that his thoughts were running parallel to hers.

He caught his breath, and she watched in fascination as his eyes slowly darkened and dropped to linger on her lips. The hand at her back moved restlessly down to the top of her hip. "God! You're going to be dangerous," he said huskily.

The deep voice was low and hypnotic and sent tiny shivers of excitement through her. When she looked up at him her eyes were slightly apprehensive, but her expression was sincere. "No. You're the one who's dangerous."

"Why?" he asked curiously.

"Because you're out of my class and—"

"Out of your class? That's a joke!"

"Why?"

"You're an intelligent woman, a talented writer, soon to be very successful indeed." He shrugged.

"But totally unsophisticated."

His lips twisted. "Sophistication is too easy to acquire and too quick to become jaded."

"Well, anyway, you're very attractive. You must know how handsome you are, Hunter, and you make me feel...different."

His soft laugh was almost embarrassed. "Do you always tell the truth so easily? Most women would tease and hide their feelings."

"Should I?"

"No!" Hunter blurted sharply. "No," he added then, more evenly. "Your guilelessness is refreshing, Gabby. Don't change."

The music ended, but Hunter kept her in a loose embrace. "Let's dance the next one." His thumb unconsciously stroked the sensitive skin inside her wrist.

"Okay," she agreed softly. She was afraid of the sensations that seemed to dart about inside her, radiating from the places he touched. This awareness needed to be tempered with lightness. "To return to the subject, last Sunday you gave me a long lecture about being too truthful," she said. "Remember Boston?"

He groaned. "Caught in my own trap. There must be a middle ground somewhere."

Gabby pretended to contemplate his remark. "Well, I suppose I could stick strictly to truisms—self-evident, obvious truths."

Hunter lifted a suspicious brow, but grinned. "I have the most horrible premonition that I shouldn't ask." His hand came up to brush a strand of hair away from her cheek. "Tell me anyway."

"Well, let's see." She pursed her lips and drew her brows together. "Euripides' first law of truth: ice cream has no bones," she said with mock seriousness.

Hunter laughed in spite of himself. "That's awful," he said, shaking his head ruefully. "I hope you don't like puns, too."

She wrinkled her nose. "I hate them. I'm only addicted to truisms. How about this one? The band is taking an intermission," she said, grinning. "That is rather obvious and self-evident."

Hunter looked around blankly to find that they stood alone on the floor with their arms around each other and several amused glances directed their way. "You witch!" He turned her and with a hand at her waist guided her off the floor. "I have one for you," he said when they reached their table. He didn't pull out her chair. Instead he took some bills from his pocket and threw them on the table.

"What is it?" she questioned.

"When we're outside," he promised with a smile.

"It had better be a good one. I'll have you know I'm a pro at this."

"It's a good one all right," he assured her.

But there was a certain grimness in his tone that made her heart beat faster. Was the pleasantry between them over?

They collected their coats and emerged into the chilly spring air. "Let's walk for a while," Hunter suggested. "Unless you're cold."

Gabby turned up the collar of the velvet cloak and shook her head. "No, I like to walk."

He tucked her hand with his into the pocket of his overcoat. She liked the warm feeling of their fingers laced together. They had gone about half a block when Gabby again sought an answer. "What's your truism, Hunter?"

He stopped and turned to her. His other hand left his pocket to trace the line of her jaw with his knuckles. She watched in fascination as his eyes darkened to jet under the light of the street lamp. "I ache to taste your mouth."

Suddenly the air between them was charged with electricity. Gabby withdrew her hand as though it had been scorched. She started to take a step backward, but he caught her shoulders.

"Th-that's not a truism," she protested weakly. "It isn't self-evident or obvious."

He was drawing her gently back into the harbor of his arms. The heat that emanated from his body shattered her strength into bits of frail longing. Her lips parted without her knowing, and her neck refused to support the weight of her head.

Just before his mouth covered hers with the first light caress he whispered, "It is to me."

To me, too, Gabby thought recklessly. His breath was warm on her lips and tasted of the fine brandy he'd had after dinner. She was drunk with him. Unwilling or unable to deny that this was what she wanted, had wanted for a long time, she lifted her arms to wind them around his neck and let him take her full weight.

A muffled groan escaped from deep in Hunter's throat as he fought the restriction of the velvet cloak to slide his hands inside along her back. They burrowed under the tunic to roam over her soft skin with long sweeping strokes. His mouth opened completely over her willing lips as though he wanted to consume her.

Had she been rational at all, Gaby thought vaguely, she would have been staggered by her response. But at the moment she was content to give herself up to sensation... to the crisp feel of his hair under her hands, the male scent of him, the taste of his tongue exploring the soft cavern of her mouth, their bodies meeting breast to thigh with burning,. intoxicating excitement.

When he finally pulled his mouth away to gasp against the soft skin of her neck, she whimpered slightly. He immediately brought a protective hand up to hold her head against his shoulder. "Gabby... Gabby..." he breathed raggedly.

"Hunter?" Her own voice was practically inaudible. She could feel his heart pound against her cheek in rhythm with the heavy beat of hers.

"I didn't know you would be like this," he murmured, his lips nibbling sensually along the curve of her neck, on the lobe of her ear.

The words sent an unexpected chill through her. She wasn't, not really. Like her mother, she was playing a role tonight. She swallowed to moisten her dry throat and pulled away as far as he would allow. Her eyes searched his, willing him to understand. This was important. "I'm still me, Hunter," she said.

He seemed to ignore her protest. "I've wanted to kiss you since the moment you stepped out of that dressing room the first time. Tonight you're half Gabby, half Lily. And they are both fascinating, bewitching." With his broad hand still spread across her cheek and tangled into her hair, he tilted her head back against his shoulder, seeking her mouth again with a hungry urgency. "And damned desirable."

The admission was grudgingly given, but Gabby had no chance to analyze it, for she was immediately drowning once more in the magic of his embrace. If she was making a mistake it was too late to rectify it now. The Great Hunter Graham was kissing her in a way she'd never been kissed before. It was enchantment, wonderful and exciting, and she wished it would go on forever.

Hunter finally brought them back to the present, gently parting their lips, placing his forehead against hers. He was taking deep steadying breaths that expanded his wide chest to crush her breasts even closer against him. His arms were like bands of iron. "I've got to get you home," he stated huskily.

Gabby gave a sigh that she felt from her toes. "Yes." But she didn't really mean it. Foolishly she wished this night would never end, sending her back, as it must, to her pragmatic world.

A cab would never have appeared so quickly had she needed one, but all Hunter had to do was lift a finger and there it was. He put her inside and joined her, reaching for her hand.

When they arrived at her mother's house, Hunter told the driver to wait and climbed out to walk her through the iron gate to the door of her apartment.

She gave him her keys and watched as he unlocked the door. "It's been a wonderful evening, Hunter. Thank you." She was amazed at how calm her voice sounded, when inside she was a churning tangle of confusing emotions.

"Gabby...." Hunter seemed to hesitate, then handed her keys back.

"What is it?" she asked as she dropped them into her purse.

He ran a hand through his hair in an awkward gesture that was very much out of character. "I didn't want to tell you until the last minute so you wouldn't worry."

Her eyes strained to see his expression in the dim light. What was wrong?

"I'll pick you up in the morning at five," he finally told her firmly. "You're going to be on 'Good Morning America.'"

"I'm what!" Gabby exclaimed.

"You heard me," he said, his mouth a straight,

grim line. "I hated to spring it on you like this, but believe me, I thought it was for the best. You would only have worried longer."

"But...but I can't! I'm not ready! No, Hunter. Please, no!"

He caught her flailing hands in both of his. "Calm down, Gabby. It's too late. Promotional spots have been playing all night on the network, announcing that you'll appear tomorrow morning. Besides, you're as ready as you'll ever be."

"I'm not," she argued desperately.

Hunter silenced her protests most effectively by pulling her into his arms and kissing her until she was almost senseless. Then he pushed her gently through the door and closed it behind her.

Gabby leaned back against the panels for a moment. Her thoughts were in a turmoil, and the least of them concerned an appearance on nationwide television. She had been right when she said that Hunter Graham was a dangerous man. One evening, one dinner, one dance, several kisses, and he had maneuvered her thoughts away from the real problem as neatly as though he'd been influencing her all her life.

"Gabby, is that you?" her mother called from her living room.

"Yes, mother," she answered, surprised. "It's late. What are you doing down here?"

"Dear, the most astounding thing! A messenger delivered an unbelievable number of the smartest-looking boxes. I had to let him in. And on television they're saying...." Her mother's voice trailed off as Gabby appeared in the door. "My heavens!" she finally exclaimed when she could speak again.

Gabby smiled, forcing aside her preoccupation with the taste of Hunter on her lips. If she had needed a confirmation that she had indeed changed her appearance, the stunned expression on her mother's face provided it amply. "Well, what do you think?" she asked.

Henrietta came slowly closer. "I think that I no longer have a little girl," she said in a plaintive, almost fearful voice.

In a blinding flash of insight Gabby realized the truth. Perhaps Henrietta didn't acknowledge it, but all these years she had been trying to keep her daughter from growing up, growing away. For a moment Gabby let her eyes fall. No. Her mother would never deliberately do such a thing, but... unconsciously? There had been just the two of them for so long, ever since the death of husband and father more than twenty years earlier. Henrietta depended on her daughter. Had she tried to make her daughter dependent on her, too, without knowing?

A quick rush of sympathy sent Gabby to put her arms around the tiny woman for a reassuring hug. "Oh, mother, maybe you don't have a little girl, but you'll always have a daughter."

Henrietta nodded. Tears glistened in her eyes. "Yes, Gabby, and I think I've suddenly realized that I should have done this for you years ago."

Gabby felt the tears sting in her own eyes at her mother's admission. She had been right. She forced herself to grin. "I probably wouldn't have agreed, you know. I was too much of a tomboy to have paid attention to clothes and makeup."

"But you're happy about it now, aren't you?" Her mother obviously couldn't believe she wouldn't be.

"I think so. Ask me again in a few months," she said with more honesty than she'd intended.

"No wonder Hunter was so angry when he found out your age. I never even noticed how young you looked before."

"Hunter! Oh, mother!" Gabby wailed, suddenly reminded. "He only told me a minute ago about the television appearance tomorrow. What am I going to do?"

"You'll be fine," her mother assured her, taking a deep steadying breath. "And now, Gabby, I have been dying to see what's in those beautiful boxes."

"Come on, then—you won't believe all the money I spent." Gabby led the way, but just before they reached her bedroom her mother stopped her with a hand on her arm. "Gabby, I do hope that when the furor has died down you'll start writing seriously."

"We'll see," said Gabby. She didn't add that she had already finished one new manuscript, taken it to the typist and begun another. Her mother would be pleased with one of them anyway.

5

WHEN THE DOORBELL RANG on the dot of five, Gabby was ready. She opened the door and sailed past Hunter with her nose in the air for about three steps, until her arm was caught and she was whirled around.

The light from the street lamp illuminated his smile just before his head came down to blot it out. His lips were cool from the early-morning air, and he tasted minty and fresh. The kiss was brief but thorough, and when he finally raised his head, her fingers were curled into the lapels of his jacket.

"Good morning, tiger," he murmured, drawing her into a closer embrace.

"Good morning," she said dazedly.

His lips played down the side of her cheek to her ear. "How are you today?" he asked, and nipped her lobe.

Gabby caught her breath at the sensation. Her pique over her restless night and the reason for it was forgotten, but ... how was she? She had no idea. "Uh, could you get back to me on that?"

He chuckled and held her away to let his eyes travel down the length of her. she had decided to wear red. The dress was a simple wrap in style, but the effect on her was anything but simple. It outlined dramatically the firm thrust of her high breasts, and the wide sash made her waist look tiny. When she moved the silken material swirled around her knees, hinting at the beautiful shape of her long legs.

The dimple in his cheek deepened. "Do you always look this good in the morning?"

The silly remark relieved the tension in Gabby, and she relaxed visibly. He took her arm and escorted her down the steps to put her into the sleek black sports car that waited at the curb.

She didn't answer until he was in the seat beside her and the car was moving down the street. He looked good, too. The tan camel's hair coat didn't disguise the breadth of his shoulders. Under it he wore a pale blue sport shirt open at the neck. Her eyes lingered on the large hands that handled the steering wheel so expertly. There were fine dark hairs across the back of them. She tried to remember if they were wiry or soft. Surely she'd touched them last night....

Jolted by the direction of her thoughts, she made an effort to answer the earlier comment lightly. "Only when I've spent an hour getting this way. How on earth do these people do it every morning?"

"They go to bed early, I imagine. Did you sleep well?" he asked.

"Not a wink," she informed him smartly. "Did you expect me to?"

"Gabby, I'm sorry." He really sounded regretful. "But if I'd told you about the show earlier you would have been even more nervous." He reached for her hand and lifted it to his lips. Silently, she thanked Marie for insisting she use that yucky cream.

As they drove through the nearly deserted streets

her thoughts returned to the ordeal she faced. "Maybe, but I don't see how I can be any more nervous than I am right now. My palms are sweaty and my knees are shaking. My heart is pounding like a jackhammer."

"Of course. I just kissed you," Hunter told her imperturbably. "It has that effect on all my women."

She caught back a gasp of indignation until she saw his grin. He was trying to joke her out of her stage fright. She was grateful for his efforts, but she certainly wasn't going to touch that statement. "I hope they have a pot of coffee going at the station," she said instead.

Just before they entered the building Gabby looked up at him, real fear in her eyes. She spoke through a constricted throat. "How many people watch this program, Hunter?"

Hunter put a warm, comforting arm around her shoulders. "Only one," he said into her hair. "Pretend it's just me you're talking to."

"Is that supposed to reassure me?" she snapped petulantly, and he laughed.

THE STUDIO was a moving, shifting tumult. An assistant producer hustled Gabby first to a makeup studio. Hunter motioned that he would wait for her and turned to speak to the famous woman who greeted half of a sleepy America every morning with a cheerful smile.

She seemed to know Hunter very well, thought Gabby with a sudden inexplicable twinge of envy. Her eyes widened. What was she thinking? She had no right being jealous of Hunter Graham and no sense at all if she let herself care for him. She didn't move in his social stratum, but for years she'd heard all the rumors and read all the gossip columns. She would not make a fool of herself over him as others had. He was playing an intriguing little game to keep her happy for now, but if she let herself read more into it than he meant, she could wind up very, very unhappy. True, she had been more stirred by his kisses than by any others she'd ever shared, but that meant only that he was a specialist in more than publishing books.

The makeup artist settled her in a chair that tilted back. She closed her eyes and found herself reliving the kisses again, particularly the first one. The sponge of the makeup artist became the featherlike touch of Hunter's fingers on her cheek; the gloss on her lips, the first teasing stroke of his mouth. This was impossible! It had to stop. She opened her eyes with a blink that ruined her mascara, and the man had to start over.

The lights were hot and blinding. Gabby was told to take deep breaths if she was nervous and not to fidget. From somewhere a copy of her book appeared. *Oh, God,* she prayed. And then it was time.

The interview didn't last long, but the red eye of the camera was ever vigilant, like a giant monster who circled and feinted, ready at any moment to move in for the kill—with Lily Andore/Gabriella Constant as its prey.

IN THE BLACKNESS beyond the camera Hunter watched as Gabby's fingers curled around the edge of her book, completely obliterating the title. He chuckled softly to himself. Those clenched fingers were the only outward sign of her nervousness. She sat effortlessly erect in the molded plastic chair. When she moved her head in response to a comment from the man who was conducting the interview, her hair swung forward to brush her cheek. Hunter remembered the silken texture of her skin under his fingers, the thickness of her hair tangled in his hand.

Frowning and annoyed with himself at the thought, he slid his hands into the pockets of his trousers and rocked back slightly on his heels. Gabriella Constant was a marketable commodity. He would do well to remember that. From the time of his father's death he had devoted all his energies to making Graham House what it was today. Women were a pleasant diversion from work, and that was sufficient for his needs. He had never allowed one to become important enough to distract him from his goals. Someday, perhaps, he might think about a family, but at thirty-four he had plenty of time.

Gabby's hand left the book to make a point in the air. Her fingers were long, he thought idly. *I wonder if she plays the piano.* And those long legs.... He jingled the change in his pocket and received a glare from a woman with a clipboard in her hand and granny glasses on her nose.

He concentrated on the dialogue for a few minutes. She was doing well. He could hardly believe that the poised young woman he watched was the same sharp-tongued ragamuffin he'd always known. Twenty-six—a good age. Abruptly he brought his thoughts up short again. *What the hell are you thinking, Graham? A good age for what?*

Still, he knew a moment's regret for the ragamuffin. He was about to shove her into a world she knew nothing about, a world in which wits counted for more than intelligence. The newfound beauty would give her a power she hadn't known—sad, but the way of the world—and it would also make her a quarry for the vultures. He felt his stomach muscles contract at the memory of how she had looked yesterday when she stepped through the curtains at Betsy's. He'd reacted as though he'd been punched—right there. Was it the eyes—those smoky, sultry gray eyes—or the mouth... full, moist, tempting? Or was it that glorious body—richly endowed, ripe? He'd never even known... and the surge of desire had been like a storm raging through the blood in his veins. Only later, when she picked up her banter again, had he regained his senses.

He sighed, earning himself another glare. Truisms, huh? It was self-evident and obvious that he'd better keep his mind on business.

WHEN IT WAS OVER Gabby couldn't remember the first word she had uttered. In fact she couldn't remember leaving the studio or getting into Hunter's car. When she recovered she found herself back in the leather seat, being driven through the early mist of dawn.

She glanced tentatively over at Hunter. He didn't seem upset, so she mustn't have said anything outrageous. Indeed, he looked pleased. He turned his head to smile at her, but she couldn't smile back. Her head was aching like thunder.

"Glad it's over?" he asked.

Would her voice work? "Yes," she said breathlessly.

"How about stopping for breakfast? Are you hungry?"

"No!" She was afraid she would throw up if she had to eat now. "No," she repeated more mildly, trying out a weak smile. "I just want to go home and go to bed."

Hunter gave her folded hands a brotherly pat. "Don't worry, honey. It gets easier every time. Before you know it you'll be an old pro in front of the camera."

She wouldn't ask him what he was talking about, not now. She didn't want to know.

THE WEEKEND PASSED PEACEFULLY, and by Sunday night Gabby was fully recovered from her ordeal and ready to get back to teaching sixteen-year-old hellions.

On Monday morning at eight o'clock she arrived at school wearing a pair of mauve wool slacks from her new wardrobe and a crisp tailored white shirt from her old one.

At nine o'clock she left again with a tear-streaked face and echoes of disparaging, reproachful remarks ringing in her ears.

The editor of the school paper, who was one of her history students, had met her at the door of her classroom with the message that Mr. Ward wanted to see her.

She didn't think anything about the summons to Steven's office until the young girl called after her, "Don't worry, Miss Constant, if they fire you we'll blow this thing sky-high in the *Sentinel*."

Gabby gave a wry smile over her shoulder. It seemed the students always knew when there was trouble before the faculty did, but she should have realized this situation wasn't going to pass unnoticed.

She could never have suspected just how bad it would be, though, even in her wildest imaginings. The principal's office was crowded to the walls. There by the window she recognized the president of the parents' club, and lounging in the principal's chair was the chairman of the school board himself. Other grim faces ringed the room as Gabby squared her shoulders and closed the door behind her.

She looked to Steven for an explanation, but his face was as closed as all the rest. Gabby felt a pang of disappointment. He seemed to be ranged with the others—against her. She considered Steven a good friend, but obviously friendship wasn't going to be allowed to color his good judgment. Poor Steven. They'd had fun together when she could coax him out of the grave solemnity that he thought should be worn like a mantle by a high-school principal.

The chairman did most of the talking, but the others did pipe up when they felt it was necessary. Gabby stood quietly and accepted it all for the first half hour or so, but anyone who knew her really well would have recognized the signs of her building temper, the clenched fists and white knuckles, the tightening of her lips, the telltale flush that colored her neck. Finally she reached the stage at which she had to either erupt or burst, and she took great pleasure in erupting.

No one in the room escaped, and when the tears spilled over they were not tears of shame or hurt but scalding hot tears of unabashed fury. The man lounging in Steven's chair was proclaimed a pompous ass; the woman by the window was told that she would forever be a prune-lipped spinster no matter how many children she had; and Steven himself was instructed with a haughty, if damp, sniff that he should start the bonfire right away so the book burning could begin.

"I'm really disappointed in you, Steven." With evil relish she went on to imply that their relationship was much closer than it actually was, taking great pleasure in the furious flush that rose to his cheeks and the suspicious glares he was receiving from the others. *Crawl your way out of that one*, she told him mentally.

When Gabby finally ran out of breath and wheeled to jerk open the door, she was greeted with applause and cheers by the large group of students gathered in the hall.

That *did* embarrass her.

WORD GOT AROUND FAST, and the telephone jangled relentlessly. First it was the teachers' union, NATS. "We'll sue," screamed the strident voice of the union leader.

Then it was the Civil Freedom Association. The lawyer was quite solemn as he rattled off one writ or code or whatever after another. Gabby wasn't listening.

The third group that wanted to take up her cause was the Proponents of Women's Rights, POWR. Of course, the female voice told her, she wouldn't be a particularly popular case with their members because her book *did* degrade women, but since she was a woman and *had* been discriminated against, they were willing to help.

She didn't hear from Steven, of course. She hadn't really expected to, but the thought made her sad and angry at the same time. She *had* warned him.

Gabby refused all offers politely but firmly. "Thank you for your suggestions, but I can take care of myself," she told them.

She had considered a lawsuit at first. It was all so unfair. But before she reached home she had dismissed that idea. Just the thought of an ordeal like that made her shudder; she was too much of a private person. The scene at school had left her feeling like a towel that had been twisted and squeezed out. A trial would be a hundred times worse.

She had just turned away from hanging up the phone when the bell rang again. It was the last straw. She jerked the receiver up and said in a very loud voice, "I don't want any help. Just leave me alone!"

That deep familiar chuckle reached her ears just before she slammed the receiver down. "Hunter?" she inquired tentatively.

"Had a rough day, honey?" he asked sympathetically.

"You don't know," she told him with asperity. "I hope you don't want to sue somebody!"

"Hell, no," he assured her. "We'd win, of course, but it would cost a bundle. No, I was wondering if you'd like to go out tonight?"

"I'd love it! Anything to get out of this house."

The sardonic note in his voice was unmistakable. "Thanks a lot."

Damn the male ego. "Thank you, Hunter. I'd love to go out with you," she said more formally.

"That's better." Now he was satisfied, but she began to wonder about her sanity. She had accepted too readily. It was folly to go out with him again. Would she be able to resist if he turned on that potent charm? The temptation would be there, definitely, but it would be awful if she made a fool of herself. She opened her mouth to renege, but before she could speak he did.

"The Knicks are in town. Do you still like basketball?"

Her brows shot up. "Yes, I do."

"Okay, I'll pick you up at seven."

A basketball game. That should be harmless enough. "I'll be ready," she told him.

BETWEEN BITES OF HOT DOG and sips of Coke, he got the whole story of the firing out of her.

Occasionally her recital was interrupted by the action on the court in front of them, but Hunter seemed more interested in her than in the game.

That was flattering, as was the way he sat with a protective arm across her shoulders. But his attentiveness was alarming, too. She was much too aware of the hard muscle next to her cheek when she turned to speak to him, much too aware of the spicy scent of his after-shave. "Even Steven didn't offer any encouragement," she finished.

"Is he the Felix Unger type I've met at your mother's a couple of times?"

She had to smile at the comparison. "I didn't realize you'd met. He doesn't come if he can help it. I think mother's friends shake him up a bit." She sighed. "Anyway, now I'm among the ranks of the unemployed."

Rather than console her with empty sympathy he took a more practical attitude. "Do you want to fight it? If so we'll—"

She interrupted quickly, "No. I really don't, Hunter. I know it was unfair and prejudicial. I've been told by the NAT, POWR, ACLU, POU and every other acronymic organization that they would be glad to help, but I just don't want to get into a lawsuit over this." She sighed. "I was ready for a change anyway. I'd been thinking of switching fields entirely. Maybe looking for a job in business."

He reached over with his napkin to wipe a spot of mustard from her chin. "What about the tour? Do you want to delay it?"

She was surprised and puzzled by the offer. "My friends think I should," she said slowly.

"Friends?"

Shrugging, she explained, "Other teachers mostly. Between calls from the acronyms this afternoon I had plenty of advice. If I keep a low profile for a while they think I'll get my job back."

"And is that what you want?" He was being very cautious, not pushing her decision at all.

As a result she made one immediately. "I don't want to go back," she said firmly, and grinned. "Cicero's law of location: no matter where you are, you are there. I may as well start from where I am and go forward." She joined in his laughter. "Why don't you speed up the tour?"

His mouth curved in a satisfied smile, showing almost all of those beautiful, straight white teeth.

For a moment she was diverted by the sight. They were sitting close, jammed in by other fans. If he moved just a couple of inches.... She blinked. From somewhere outside herself came a niggling voice that told her she had just been neatly maneuvered, but she decided she didn't care.

"I wish you wouldn't look at my mouth like that," Hunter murmured.

"Like what?" she breathed, finally prying her gaze away to lift her eyes to his.

He caught his breath, then shifted positions with a strange restless movement.

Her eyes dropped in embarrassment. It must have looked as if she were deliberately tempting him to kiss her.

"Gabby, look at me." She obeyed "Did Steven hurt you badly?" he asked gently.

"Steven?" She had to think a minute. "Yes...because he didn't stand up for me."

"Is that the only reason?" he persisted.

"I had warned him about Lily," she offered. What was he talking about?

He shook his head. "I meant...are you in love with him?"

"Of course not!" Resolutely she returned her attention to the ball game and so missed the glitter in the dark eyes.

"I'll start the preparations for the tour tomorrow. Where do you want to go first?" he asked briskly.

"Boston?" she suggested immediately with a wry smile.

He chuckled, but had the grace to look embarrassed. "I was only threatening you because I was so angry that day. You don't even have to *go* to Boston, Gabby," he said seriously.

"May as well get it over with," she told him. "I shall courageously restore the reputation of Graham House in Beantown. And in the meantime, may I have another hot dog?"

6

QUOTATIONS FROM THE RADIO SHOW and the television interview, rather than mollifying a clamoring public, only whetted their insatiable appetite for more and more information about Lily Andore. In the next weeks gears were shifted into overdrive. Boston was the first stop on Gabby's promotional tour, and surprisingly everything went well.

She received a warmer welcome than expected and found herself enjoying the attention. Especially since Hunter made the two-day trip with her.

The schedule was hectic and there wasn't time for them to be alone together. She wasn't sure whether she should mourn that fact or celebrate it. But just knowing that he was near gave Gabby the boost of self-confidence she needed. She didn't take the time to analyze her reliance on his presence until they were on the plane returning to New York.

Hunter pulled a sheaf of papers from his briefcase and gave them to her. "Here is your schedule for the first part of the tour. Unfortunately, Bev, our publicist is out of commission with the flu. But I'm very pleased with the way you handled yourself in Boston, Gabby. You're going to be fine."

She took the papers and began to leaf through them. Philadelphia, Chicago, San Francisco, Dallas, New Orleans, Miami, Atlanta, Washington. Forcing a brightness into her voice that she didn't feel, she turned to smile at him. "So, I'm on my own for now?"

"Until Bev gets back," he agreed. "You aren't afraid, are you?"

"Afraid? Of course not," she scoffed. But deep inside she knew she was lying. She had done well in Boston, but with the secure feeling that Hunter was near, that had been easy. She finally had to face the fact that Hunter Graham was becoming important to her, more important than any man had ever been before. And to him she was a piece of merchandisable material who had to be kept happy.

He had been there when she needed him, his support sustaining her the morning she'd appeared on television, the day she'd been fired from her job and on this trip to Boston. But he was letting her know that the support was being withdrawn. He couldn't hold her hand any longer. She would have to plunge into the icy waters of publicity totally alone now.

It was for the best, she decided. To become emotionally involved with Hunter wouldn't do at all. The kisses they had shared were too electrifying to be ignored.

He must have realized that, too, because the last few times they had been together he'd treated her more like a kid sister. However, she had an uneasy feeling that the memory of those kisses would be enough to send her carelessly into his arms if he should beckon.

He was a physical man. His arm often rested casually across her shoulders, and he always guided her with a large hand in the small of her back. She felt a permanent warmth in that spot. Occasionally he would reach for her eager hand.

It would definitely be better if she followed his lead and treated him with the same casual friendliness that he'd shown recently. She could do it, she vowed silently.

She forced her concentration to the sheets in her lap and asked a few pertinent questions about the tour. When she met his eyes, though, there was a strange gleam there, a sparkle of amusement... tinged with something that looked like regret.

Trying not to squirm under that intense regard, she said gaily, "So I'm off to Philadelphia, with hardly a chance to do laundry!"

"Yes, off to Philadelphia." His answer was almost distracted.

She could do it, she repeated to herself, over and over.

WHEN GABBY ARRIVED IN PHILADELPHIA two days later, her bubble of confidence burst with a vengeance. The taxi she took from the train station deposited her in the middle of a picket line in front of her hotel. She looked around to locate the object of the demonstration and found herself staring at a placard bearing the name of Gabriella Constant/Lily Andore.

"What on earth...?" She gaped blankly at the woman who waved a sign in her face.

"There she is!" The pickets surged forward. "You're a traitor to your sex! Coward!" Screams echoed in her ears as a quick-thinking doorman took her arm and cleared a path.

"I'll get your luggage," he shouted, pushing her

through the huge double doors toward the registra-
tion desk. The manager took over from there, hus-
tling her into a waiting elevator while the doorman
waded back into the crowd. When the heavy doors
slid shut, closing them in, she turned a frantic face to
the man with her.

"What is going *on*?" she demanded.

The grim-faced man handed her a newspaper.
"You can read all about it in here. Page four-A. And
please, next time would you stay someplace else?"

Encumbered by a tote bag, her purse and an all-
weather coat, Gabby had to content herself with accepting the paper for now. The doors soon opened
onto a carpeted hallway, and she followed meekly as
the man led her to a door and unlocked it.

He lingered only long enough to assure her that
her luggage would be up shortly. Then he closed her
inside the luxurious suite with the suggestion that
she have dinner up there. She didn't miss a step but
continued through the living room into the bedroom.

Dropping everything else on the kingsize bed, she
quickly opened the paper to page four-A. A picture
of herself as she had appeared on the morning show
faced a rather fuzzy photograph of another woman.
She scanned the article with growing disbelief before
going back to read every word more carefully.

It would appear that the woman representing
POWR, Proponents of Women's Rights, who had
called Gabby on the day of her firing had been busy.
She had made a statement to the press outlining
POWR's offer of assistance in helping her regain her
job. But, instead of relating the true reason for
Gabby's refusal, she had made it sound as if Gabby

had declined the organization's help because she didn't believe in women's rights.

Kicking off her shoes, Gabby climbed on the huge bed and hitched her legs up to sit cross-legged. With the paper spread out in front of her she proceeded to read the article for the third time.

"I can't believe you would deliberately lie," she told the woman whose picture stared up at her from the sheet. She knew that her cause would never have been really popular with the group, and that was another reason to beg off; but it appeared that a fringe element had taken over her case, and those involved were determined to milk every possible bit of publicity from the incident.

Harsh words leaped out at her:

What else could you expect from someone who would write a book so demeaning to women? Nevertheless Gabriella Constant, a.k.a. Lily Andore, has set back women in education by years because she refuses to fight this. She should go all the way to the Supreme Court if necessary.

Gabby could almost hear the voice on the telephone now that she had a face to put with it. She growled a word that would have turned her mother's ears red and threw the newspaper across the room. With an angry glower she watched the sheets spread and float to the floor. Dammit! They were using her to get media exposure for themselves.

The telephone rang and she snatched it up. "Hello!" she snapped.

"I see you've heard," said the deep voice.

"Heard? My God, Hunter, I had to wade through

a picket line to get inside the hotel! She lied! Why did she lie?"

"Calm down, tiger. Maybe she misunderstood you."

Gabby had to take a deep breath before she could answer. How could he take the side of that woman? "And this sells more books, right?" She finally suggested in a saccharine-sweet voice, "Maybe *you* planted the story."

"Don't be childish! Of course I didn't plant it." He sounded even more impatient than she felt.

She counted to ten. "I'm sorry. I didn't mean that." Her head dropped, sending her hair forward to curtain her face as she traced the pattern on the spread with a finger.

"As a matter of fact, it looks suspiciously like a media event."

Her head came up with a jerk. "But how did they know which hotel?"

"No, Gabby. My office did not announce where you'd be staying," Hunter said firmly. "Our regional sales director called me. POWR reported their plans to picket your arrival in the morning newspaper. He was delighted."

Had he read her thoughts? She relaxed. "I didn't really think...."

"Oh, yes, you did. But I forgive you," he said lightly.

She had to smile. She put a hand to her breast dramatically, as if he could see. "Thank you! The Great Hunter Graham forgives me. I'm overwhelmed!"

He laughed. She could visualize the crinkles at the edge of his eyes, his white teeth gleaming in the tanned face.

"You're as bad as your mother, tiger. Do you want me to come out?" he added in a deeper tone that almost sounded wishful.

Catching her lower lip between her teeth, she shook her head. "No, I won't need you, Hunter. I'm fine. After all, this is the City of Brotherly Love."

"I've been thinking," he said after a brief silence. "The hotel's management probably put the story out. Everyone likes publicity and you *are* news."

She laughed. "Well, it certainly backfired. You should have seen that poor manager's face." Suddenly her back stiffened with indignation. "The management? How dared they? Hunter, that man told me never to stay here again... and I was more or less ordered to have dinner in my room!"

"So what are you going to do?" he asked mildly.

"Make a grand entrance into the main dining room, of course. What did you assume I would do?"

That deep chuckle indicated his approval, but then he suddenly was all business. "The sales director will call for you at eight. He wants to take you to dinner. That way you won't have to face them alone."

I wish it were you. "Thank you. Is he married?" she couldn't resist teasing.

She could hear the frown in his voice. "No," he said bluntly and hung up.

She looked at the dead receiver in her hand for a minute. Then she hung up and fell back on the bed to stare at the white ceiling.

Was Hunter jealous? No. She would not permit herself to hope that he even cared.

She twisted restlessly. Hope. Was that what she felt? Suddenly she was still. She let her mind drift back over the ten years she'd known Hunter. She had always been the one who initiated their minor conflicts, she realized with some surprise. The barbs, the sarcastic remarks—had they been a way of gaining his attention? The book itself—was that why she'd written it?

The girl Gabby was and the woman she'd become warred within, leaving her confused and unsettled.

If she'd wanted Hunter to notice her as a woman, why had she fought so strenuously against the makeover? Subconsciously had she protected herself from a possible rejection? If she looked her best and Hunter still didn't notice her it would be worse, much worse, than being treated with amused indulgence.

She lifted agitated fingers to comb through her hair and sat up. Her thoughts were so illogical right now. Nothing made sense. Those women who paced downstairs.... But they were not the problem and she knew it. The problem was the black-haired, black-eyed spirit of masculinity whose face swam before her. Now she was forced to admit the crush she'd had on him since she was sixteen, a silly teenage crush that had lingered well into her twenties. Well, surely she could handle an unrealistic attraction like that.

With a feverish burst of energy she jumped off the bed. She unpacked quickly, stripped off the traveling suit and took a cool refreshing shower. Naked, she returned to the bedroom and picked up the telephone. "This is Miss Constant in room six-eleven. I'd like you to hold all calls, please." Then she slid between the crisp sheets and closed her eyes determinedly.

THE PHILADELPHIA VISIT was to last three days. After the scene in front of the hotel, the next two days were relatively quiet. Gabby visited shopping malls and bookstores in the area and signed her name hundreds of times, trying not to think about how lonely she felt.

On the third day she was to appear on a talk show hosted by a well-known spokesman for women's rights. It was a foregone conclusion that he would bring up the subject again. The session would not be a pleasant one, but Gabby promised herself staunchly that she would not lose her temper. Even so in the taxi, on the way to the studio, she felt the familiar stirrings of panic. This wasn't simply a news interview lasting only a few minutes. This show ran for a full hour and was syndicated all over the country.

The host was articulate and acutely perceptive. She had watched the program a few times and was fully convinced that the man could smell fear.

Well, she told herself as her cab reached the studio, there was nothing to be done but face the ordeal as bravely as possible. She resolved to be calm and composed and explain her position in a rational manner.

What she hadn't counted on was the man's fondness for hearing himself talk. Afterward she tried to remember if there was even one sentence she'd been allowed to finish.

The program had begun with a discussion of her book. The host had been fairly pleasant, inviting the members of his studio audience to participate.

Gabby was surprised at the number of questions that were sympathetic, interspersed with others filled with veiled sarcasm. But she could handle the subtle attacks. She began to relax.

Suddenly a woman in the front row piped up with, "What does your mother think of your book?"

Gabby was genuinely perplexed. "My mother?" she said blankly.

"Your mother is Henrietta Constant, isn't she?" The host of the show threw in the question.

"Well, yes, but she writes a different kind of book. She's a poet," Gabby explained.

"And you changed your name so that you wouldn't embarrass her?" he prodded.

"Well, no. Lots of authors—"

"Surely, Miss Constant, you don't call yourself an author?" He pretended horror. "Let's take another question." He pointed to another woman in the audience.

"Why are you against women having their rightful place in the world?"

"I'm not, I just—"

"Don't you have a drinking problem?"

"A *what*? Why—"

"How many men did you have to sleep with for your research?"

"I don't—"

The questions came at her from all sides. Her head swung wildly back and forth and finally she swiveled in her chair to fix the smiling man with a glare. "Are you going to stop this?"

"Why, Miss Constant, surely the public has a right to know," he told her with a sneer.

"This is a deliberate smear, and if you don't take charge of this program immediately you're going to find yourself without a guest!"

"You can't walk out." A disbelieving look slid onto his face.

"Short of tying me to the chair, I don't see how you could stop me!" she stormed. "You're trying to use me, but I'm not a crusader. This is a perfect example of how a few fanatics can ruin a wonderful idea."

"What are you referring to, the women's movement? You've done more damage than any of these sincere people." He indicated his audience with a dramatic sweep of his hand. "If you had fought for the right to keep your job...."

He let his voice trail off sadly and with a shrug turned to the camera in a movement that was so typical of his manner that she cringed. How often had she watched this program and seen that same body language? It was a clear signal that he was about to leave her to it. The sign that the gloves were off, the pretense at politeness was over, the Christians were about to be thrown to the lions. He would wait until the end of the program to symbolically turn his thumb down, but everyone in the audience—in the studio and watching the television—knew that it was only a formality.

Gabby was in full temper now, and she wasn't about to let him get away with this. "Choice!" she yelled, and the microphone gave a protesting squeal.

"What?" the man asked, taken completely by surprise.

She got to her feet. For the first time in her life Gabby was grateful for her height and her high heels. When the astonished man stumbled from his chair to face her she had the advantage of two inches. She drew herself to her full six feet and gave him her most intimidating stare.

"In case it missed your attention, that is what the

movement for equal rights is all about—the freedom
of choice for women. And at the moment I do not
choose to stay here and be massacred."

The host threw up a hand as though to stop her,
but she slapped it away. Frantically he turned to the
camera. "We'll be back after this message from our
sponsor."

As she swung around to leave, Gabby was more
than satisfied to hear that his voice had risen a full
octave. The camera followed her all the way. No red
light glowed, but she was past caring whether it was
on or not. She marched regally across the stage and
straight into the arms of Hunter Graham.

"Hunter?" she murmured, not believing. She
moved a step away from the apparition, but kept her
hands on his forearms just in case.

"Easy, tiger."

It *was* Hunter. She met his warm gaze with the
greatest feeling of relief she'd ever known. Her anger
dissipated like snowflakes in the rain. He looked
wonderful, big and confident and sexy. "Hunter...it
is you."

The hands at her waist urged her forward and he
smiled tenderly. "Yep."

She flung her arms around his neck, reveling in
the convulsive embrace that threatened to squeeze
all the breath from her lungs, then leaned back to
look up at his face in wonder.

His head dipped a scant inch. She thought he was
going to kiss her, but he pulled back sharply. Then,
as though he couldn't help himself, he gathered her
against him, crushing her lips under his with a
hunger she could feel and taste, a hunger that mag-
nified her own a thousandfold.

They clung together, sharing their heat, their energy, giving all of their resources and support to each other in this hypersensitive moment. The studio, the audience, the obnoxious host were forgotten in the joy of physical closeness, the enchantment of holding what their empty arms had longed to hold.

Too soon the kiss ended, but Hunter didn't ease his grasp. He inhaled, long and deep, and rested his forehead against hers. "I hope to hell this break is sixty seconds and not thirty."

His voice was as unsteady as Gabby's knees. "Me, too. Oh, Hunter, I'm so glad you're here." She laughed weakly and tried to pull away, belatedly realizing where they were, but he still wouldn't release her completely.

His expression was oddly unsure and almost apologetic. "I'll see you back at the hotel, sweetheart." He gave her another quick kiss and finally handed her into the arms of Daphne who hovered nearby.

The emotion of the past few minutes had left Gabby vulnerable and raw. She didn't understand what he meant and watched blankly as he straightened his tie and smoothed a hand through his dark hair. Then he turned and walked calmly over to the stage where she had been sitting.

"I hope you'll accept a last-minute substitute," he told the audience of women with a trace of that warm sensuous smile.

Through her dazed eyes Gabby could practically see their antagonism dissolve. So much for rabid feminism.

The host of the show gave Gabby one final glare before offering Hunter the empty seat beside him with a wave of his hand. He was less than pleased. "Certainly, Mr. Graham," he said with false heartiness. "I hope you're in better control of yourself than your writer."

Hunter waved his hand in a dismissive gesture. "You know how unstable artists are."

Gabby was brought rudely back down to earth. She would have marched right back up there to take exception to that statement, but Daphne had the presence of mind to hustle her out of the studio with the greatest possible speed.

BACK AT THE HOTEL she was still pacing angrily when Hunter let himself into her suite. "How dared you apologize for me to that...that bastard!" she erupted. Her hands were clenched fists planted on her hips. "He was abominable to me. He didn't deserve an apology, he deserved a black eye. If you were any kind of friend you would've given him one."

Hunter was in no mood to cope with her anger at this moment. He had passed the point where he could give her a calm lecture on discretion.

For three days he had been in constant communication with his sales director. If Gabby thought that the acrimony of the group from POWR had settled, he knew better.

At first he'd been amused. A million dollars' worth of advertising couldn't have given her the exposure she was receiving, and the sales of *Captive of Her Bed* were skyrocketing. He'd been approached by a network executive about a possible miniseries, suitably laundered, of course. Lily Andore was a phenomenon the likes of which every publisher dreams—beautiful, sexy as hell and confident.

But then as more information had filtered back to the New York office, he'd begun to have misgivings. There were members of POWR, as in every worthy organization, whose beliefs had accelerated to the fanatic. He'd seen them on the evening news, their faces distorted with hatred for anyone who didn't agree with them one hundred percent.

Gabby's high profile made her a prime target for a crank, and he was worried about her personal safety. He tried to tell himself that what he felt was a grudging responsibility because she was Henrietta's daughter. Never mind that her lips were as sweet as he'd ever tasted, that her body and his fit together so perfectly, that the scent of wild flowers in her hair lingered in his nostrils long after she was gone.

He'd decided to drive to Philadelphia to assess the situation for himself. As he'd stood behind the camera watching, his disquiet had grown. The hostility of the audience had been like a gathering storm, dark and forbidding. He could tell that Gabby was unaware of just how serious the situation was. When she marched off that stage he'd never been so relieved in his life, or so proud. She was one hell of a woman. But the conflict had to be defused, and quickly. So he'd done what had to be done.

Excusing Gabby on the grounds of artistic temperament had been a low blow, he admitted. In fact he realized that the woman he'd described was more Henrietta than her daughter. However, he'd gone into great detail to paint a word picture of a mythical, moody and touchy tragedienne.

The host and his audience had finally been mollified, but God help him if Gabby ever found out. He'd had an idea that she wouldn't be flattered even if he explained his fears for her.

He'd left the studio an hour later in none too placid a frame of mind, and when Gabby greeted him in the suite with her tirade he responded with a growing fury he couldn't explain. The sight of her breasts straining against the flimsy fabric didn't calm him at all. Or those lips, even thinned to an angry line....

Why didn't he leave her to it, he asked himself ferociously. It sold books!

"If you had sat still and ignored the enmity it would have been much more effective, Gabby! As it is, you've given the man food for several more shows, and made him out a martyr, as well," he finally blasted back. "You can't control yourself for three days!"

"I can when I'm not being lambasted for something that's not my fault! What are you doing here anyway? Surely you and Daphne have more important things to do." God, she was glorious! That gold dress clinging to her curves suggested a yearning sensuality as she flung her arms wide.

Despite his exasperation he felt the awakening of desire, and the sensation fueled his wrath further. "You're damned right we do! We have a business to run, in case you've forgotten, but instead I have to drive down here to rescue a child who can't keep her mouth shut!" Why was he bellowing at her when what he really wanted was to haul her into the bedroom and make love to her until neither of them could speak at all?

"I told you I didn't need you!" Gabby shouted,

planting her fists on her hips. She whirled away. "Why don't you leave?" she wailed.

Was she crying? He didn't know what he would do if she cried. It had been an emotion-charged morning, and he would probably put a fist through the wall. "I intend to." He glanced at his watch. "In about ten minutes. I'm leaving Daphne with you for the Chicago and San Francisco legs. If you can't grow up and learn to control yourself there, I'll cancel the tour, and neither you *nor* your mother will ever get another thing published by Graham House!"

"My mother? Why pick on her?" She glared over her shoulder at him, those mysterious eyes partially screened by her thick lashes.

He heard his voice drop dangerously low. "I publish your mother because my father did. You don't think I make any money on poetry, do you?"

Slowly she turned to face him again. She wasn't crying, but she was pale. "Mother's books give a certain prestige to the house, don't they? To make up for the other trash you publish?"

She bit on her lower lip as though to take back the words.

There was a dead silence in the room. The gray eyes, flashing silver, clashed with his own. His hand shot out to grab her arm, but when he saw her wince he dropped it with a feeling of revulsion for his behavior. What was wrong with him?

"You said it, honey; I didn't," he told her quietly. Then he turned and left.

As he went out the door Daphne came in looking over her shoulder at her employer. "What on earth...?"

Then she saw Gabby, took in the pain-filled eyes and
wan cheeks. She stepped forward, closing the door
softly behind her. "Gabby?"

Gabby took a long shuddering breath. Had she
really said such horrible things to Hunter? Tears
stung and Gabby didn't try to stop their flow. She
collapsed in Daphne's arms, sobs shaking her body,
deep racking sobs. She was crying and speaking in-
coherently. "Oh, Daphne...why did I say that? Is it
trash? He came all the way...."

"Hush, sweetie," Daphne consoled her. "Come
on. Let's sit down."

Gabby allowed herself to be steered to the sofa.
"Why did he come?" she gulped when the sobs had
quieted.

"He came because he was worried about you,"
Daphne said plainly.

"He hung up on me," Gabby sniffed. "The first
day I was here."

"I know," the older woman chuckled. "He was
raving mad for the rest of the afternoon, but when
he calmed down he was still worried."

"He was?" The silver gaze was washed with tears
but hopeful. Then she remembered. "He rescued me
from that awful man, and I screamed at him," she
wailed.

"You were upset."

"So was he." A remnant of her belligerence lingered, much to her surprise.

"Men don't like scenes, dear," Daphne explained.

Gabby choked out a laugh. "That's a truism if I
ever heard one."

"A what?" Daphne looked blank.

"You know, something that's so true it's almost ridiculous to say it out loud."

Daphne laughed. "And with a man like Hunter Graham, even more so."

Gabby risked a glance at Daphne's smile. "Has he ever been in love?" she ventured carefully.

"Heavens, no!" said Daphne. Then her gaze narrowed on Gabby's profile. "You're not falling in love with him, are you?"

"Heavens, no!" Gabby parroted her exclamation.

"Good! Because I'd hate you to be hurt, Gabby." Her brows knit in a frown. "Though I must say, I've never seen him react so strongly to any woman before. Usually he's either charming or indifferent."

"And with me his feelings are either indulgent or infuriated," Gabby agreed.

Daphne looked at her suddenly with an unreadable expression. "Yes-s." She drew the word out thoughtfully.

Gabby got to her feet. She was so tired, bone-deep, but this damn show had to go on. "Well, let's pack," she said. "I hate to admit that I might need a baby-sitter, but I'm glad you're going with me to Chicago and the coast."

"So am I. I'm sorry Bev still has the flu, but I love the food in San Francisco." Daphne looked down at her slight form. "Maybe I'll just get fat," she teased, and Gabby laughed as she was supposed to.

"Then I'll have to drag you to see Jacques and Marie," Gabby threatened.

"Oh, no! Not me!"

7

WHY HAD SHE DONE IT, Gabby wondered as she settled back in the taxi that was taking her to the airport in New Orleans.

Last night on a local program that preceded the evening news the woman who interviewed her had been particularly probing with her questions, prefacing most of them with innuendo about Lily Andore's morals.

Gabby had been quite successful in learning how to cope with antagonism. Since the debacle in Philadelphia she'd been almost overly cautious. But New Orleans wasn't exactly the capital of the Bible Belt. She had smiled politely, as Daphne had warned her to do, and mouthed meaningless phrases in response to the woman's interrogation. But the questions had grown more and more pointed until finally she was confronted with the most personal query of all.

"Miss Andore, your historical research has been quite thorough, but what about Valentine Semmes? You've written one of the sexiest characters in years, and you won't even give us a hint about your love life or *that* research. You almost sound as though you'd like our viewers to believe you're a virgin, for heavens sake!" the woman had simpered.

Gabby had raised her chin to an effective angle and fixed the woman with an impassive gaze. "I doubt that it's any of your business, but that's exactly what I am,'' she said very softly.

There was a deathly silence on the set and then all of a sudden it was broken off-camera by a husky male laugh that held a definite note of excitement. Gabby had tried to peer beyond the lights, but she couldn't see anyone.

It had taken only a moment for the woman to recover. She patted her hair and gave a nervous titter. "You don't expect us to accept that, do you? Particularly those of us who've read your book?"

"I don't really care whether you accept it or not. Nevertheless it's true."

The poor woman had been so upset that Gabby almost laughed. Her interview wasn't going at all as she had planned or she would have guarded her tongue, Gabby was sure; but the only question she seemed able to come up with then was a stunned, "But why?"

Gabby had shrugged with seeming unconcern. "I've never really thought about it. I suppose I've never met a man who could live up to my fantasies of a real hero." *And may the Lord forgive me for lying,* she'd added to herself. *Hunter Graham is more man than Valentine Semmes ever met in her three-hundred-page life!*

"Ah, er, how much longer will you be in New Orleans, Miss Andore?" The woman was filling time now.

She is probably as anxious to get this over with as I am. Gabby had tried to look properly regretful. "I'm afraid I have to leave tomorrow for Atlanta."

"Well, we certainly hope you'll come back when your next bestseller hits the stands."

Over my dead body, thought Gabby. "I'd love that," she said.

The woman had turned to the camera with a bright insincere smile. "This is Monica Bevins with your nightly Crescent City Interview. Tune in tomorrow when...."

Gabby tuned out. With a mental apology to Daphne, she tried to anticipate Hunter's reaction to this incident. At least she had controlled her temper outwardly. Besides, it wasn't anything to be ashamed of, was it?

Hunter's assistant had pronounced Gabby able to cope after a good showing in San Francisco and returned to New York. Gabby had flown on alone to Texas.

A one-day stop, Dallas had gone more smoothly than any on her tour so far. There was a lot to be said for Texas hospitality, but she missed the companionship of the older woman.

They had gone shopping together in Chicago and stuffed themselves on seafood at Fisherman's Wharf in San Francisco. Daphne was a close acquaintance of her mother's, and though Gabby had always liked her she'd been in awe of her sophisticated air. Now she'd discovered a warm and motherly side to Daphne, too.

Daphne was also discreet. Casual questions about her employer received only casual answers. Still, when she left, the loneliness had once again set in. Later that evening the dining room of the Old Orleans Hotel had become strangely silent when Gabby hesitated at the door. Did everyone in New Orleans watch that silly woman's show? She'd wished that someone was there so she wouldn't have to eat alone. She didn't put a name to the some-one, but Hunter was becoming a stronger fixation than he should have been. Often she didn't even have to close her eyes for his face to appear in her thoughts.

Should she have taken up Henrietta's offer to fly down? They talked often on the telephone, and she knew that her mother was following the tour with avid interest, keeping score on the number of books that were sold. She had astounded Gabby with the figure of two hundred fifty thousand and seemed to have given grudging approval to Lily Andore.

When Gabby voiced her surprise at the interest her mother was taking, Henrietta had answered blithely, "I was just jealous before. After all, dear, the print run on my little tomes has never been more than four thousand, and I've written eleven of them!"

Gabby bit back a chuckle. "And now your rebel of a daughter is doing pretty well the first time out."

"Pretty well? You're fantastic!"

Remembering her mother's words with a rather dry throat, Gabby had smiled at the maître d' and walked stiffly to her table. In solitary splendor she proceeded to order a most delicious meal. Only she knew that every bite tasted like cardboard.

GABBY HANDED HER BOARDING PASS to the flight atten-dant.

"Good afternoon," the young woman greeted her. "We'll be serving drinks and a snack as soon as we take off. Have a nice flight."

Gabby nodded and sank gratefully into the first-class window seat that had been indicated. She buckled her seat belt, checked her watch and, closing her eyes with a sigh, laid her head against the seat back. The plane would arrive in Atlanta at four-thirty. She was looking forward to a hot shower and bed. It had already been a long day with two signings behind her.

The noise of the plane filling with passengers was a background for her thoughts. Hunter wasn't going to like this development. What kind of a romance writer was a virgin at twenty-six? It didn't fit the image at all. Oh, what difference did it make? Gabby was tired of being an image. On a day like this, she even began to wonder who she really was. Gabby Constant or Lily Andore? Or someone in between? She'd learned in the past month that she wasn't an extension of her mother. She could be attractive and talented in her own right, and she really liked the feeling.

Someone slid into the seat beside her, and she shifted slightly closer to the window. She would have to begin looking for another job. Maybe even in another state. Or could she make enough writing full-time? The engines revved to an angry level, and the plane finally began to move.

One thing she was going to do when this tour was over was treat herself to a long vacation. She'd always wanted to go to Alaska. In the summer the weather should be pleasant, she mused. There were even cruises that sailed up from Seattle. Her lips curved into a smile at the prospect.

"I'm glad you can find something to smile about," a grim voice said beside her.

She would have known that voice anywhere. Her eyes flew open, closed tightly and opened again. "Hunter!" she said softly, not able to believe her eyes.

"Right the first time." His reply was sour.

She was startled, but not so much that his irritability didn't register. She hadn't seen him in two weeks, but his mood hadn't improved at all in that time. In fact, it seemed to have worsened. How could he possibly know? The show had only aired the previous night.

The tailored gray suit fit his broad shoulders perfectly, and the crisp white shirt emphasized his tan. He had loosened the maroon tie, and his long muscular legs were stretched out in front of him in a relaxed attitude, while he stared at the seat in front of him.

She felt an almost overwhelming urge to smooth back the dark hair where it had fallen forward on his forehead. His lips wore a sensual curve that wasn't a smile but was just as exciting. He was as sexy as ever, she thought with a sigh. "Why aren't you in New York?" she asked in a voice made husky by his nearness.

His eyes narrowed as he flicked her a careless glance. "I flew in this morning. I thought you might need me."

Gabby could tell that he didn't like to make the admission. "Why would I need anyone?" she returned in a lighter tone.

His large body had been stiffly upright, but now he moved his seat back a notch, pulled at his tie to loosen it further and opened the top button of his shirt. "Perhaps I misunderstood my representative in New Orleans. He said that your mouth had made trouble for you again," he said flatly.

"Then you know."

"Yes," he answered. "Did you tell that woman the truth?" he asked skeptically.

"Yes," she admitted quietly.

His eyes were on her now, seeking, but he wouldn't ask.

She sighed. "There are hundreds of women for every man in New York City. Can you see the male population beating down the door of Gabby Constant?"

"Didn't Henrietta tell me that you were once engaged?" He clearly still didn't believe her.

She waved a hand. "That only lasted a few days. I helped him pass American History." Meeting his eyes, she tried a smile. "The only Lincoln he knew was a town car."

He turned his face away again. The dimple in his cheek was a deep gash, but from an expression of exasperation, rather than a smile.

Gabby really ached to trace it with her finger, but that wouldn't do. She was one of his authors, that's all. He mustn't know how he bothered her. She clenched her fingers in her lap. "Why are you concerned? It sells—"

"Books!" he interrupted. "I know." His head turned and his eyes met hers, releasing the angry glare he'd tried to disguise.

What was wrong with him? "Have I ruined the tour?" she asked.

"What the hell are you talking about?"

"The tour, the image, all of it." She spread her hands hopelessly. "I know I haven't lived up to what you made me. Who wants to come and see a twenty-six-year-old virgin?"

"Dammit, Gabby! Why do you let yourself respond to those turkeys?"

"Turkeys?"

"The interviewers," he explained impatiently. "Don't you care at all about your reputation? Your own well-being?"

She shook her head to clear it. "I don't understand. What bearing...? The publicity campaign—"

"You silly little fool! I'm not mad because of a damned publicity campaign!"

"Hunter, lower your voice," she told him. He was almost shouting and the other first-class passengers stared openly.

He did, with obvious effort. "Don't you know what you've done?" he asked incredulously.

"What?" she whispered. If he wasn't angry about the tour, then what...?

"You, Miss Lily Andore, have set yourself up as a challenge for every red-blooded bachelor in the country! And probably quite a few married men, too. Each one will be fantasizing that he could be the one to deflower the notorious Lily Andore. If you let your guard down for a minute one will certainly be standing by to try."

Gabby's mouth fell open.

"No comment?" he asked nastily.

"But I didn't!" She straightened in her seat. The denial was heated. She was ready for battle. "How could you think such a thing?"

"Can I get you something?" the flight attendant interrupted, leaning over them. Her voice was deliberately low and sexy and her appreciative eyes on Hunter said even more as she brushed his shoulder with her own.

Gabby was startled at her own urge to reach across Hunter and push the woman away, but evidently he was enjoying the attention. He smiled at the woman.

"I'll have a Bloody Mary," said Gabby sharply, though she hadn't been asked.

Hunter's head swiveled. Gabby received the remnants of the smile. "And I'll have Scotch and water," he told the stewardess, but his eyes didn't leave Gabby's.

"Now," demanded Gabby, trying to put force in her voice under the spell of that dark gaze. "Where did you get such a crazy idea?"

His eyes dropped to her mouth and stayed there for a time. When they moved farther downward to her breasts she was horrified to feel her nipples harden and press against their suddenly abrasive covering. The sensation was like a callused thumb, circling, stroking. Oh, God. Could he see?

"The idea came from personal experience," he told her huskily. "You're looking lovely today, Gabby. I like that dress."

She'd forgotten what she was wearing. She looked blankly down at the lavender silk sheath. "Thank you," she mouthed, but no sound came out.

"Are you cold?" He shifted, leaned forward, his elbows on the padded armrest between them. His hands dangled on her side of the barrier, dangerously near her thigh, and his shoulders blocked her from view of the aisle.

Damn! Of course he could see. He knew exactly what he was doing to her. "No," she told him quickly, and then realized what an admission that was. If only she couldn't smell the tangy after-shave he wore, she was sure she wouldn't be so affected by his nearness, or the warmth of his gaze as it traveled over her. It was as though he were making love to her, stripping her bare, touching her without ever moving. "Hunter, please...."

Slowly one long finger came up to touch her nipple. It was the barest, lightest brush, but suddenly electric shock radiated throughout her body from that spot. She grabbed his wrist. "No!" she whispered.

"No? I thought you said 'please.'"

"Damn you. You know that isn't what I meant." Her head fell back against the seat and she turned to face him, looking up helplessly into his dark eyes.

With a twist of his wrist he laced their fingers together tightly and brought them against his chest, tugging her closer. His voice was deep and husky when he spoke. "Your lips are like a magnet. Every time I'm near you, I'm drawn to their softness. Come here, sweetheart, and kiss me."

Gabby had no intention of refusing the tender command. She wanted to taste his mouth as much as she'd ever wanted anything in her life. She let her eyes drift shut and her lips parted on a sigh.

Hunter chuckled softly, his breath stirring her senses even before she felt his lips begin to sip at hers. His tongue slid inside her upper lip and across her teeth, playing with her, teasing. While it was a delightful sensation, it had been too long since he'd kissed her, and it wasn't enough for Gabby.

She raked her free hand into his hair and brought his head down, demanding more. Hunter obliged with a swiftness that obliterated her reason. His tongue plunged into her mouth, thrusting, withdrawing, thrusting again in a duel with the willing adversary it found there. The desire that flamed so spontaneously was totally, passionately exciting.

His hand tangled in her hair, caressing her scalp with convulsive fingers, until finally he broke off the kiss in desperation. "Gabby...Gabby," he moaned softly against her lips when he could speak. "I want you, darling."

His voice was hypnotic, conjuring up wonderful pictures, pictures that Gabby could see herself.

"I'm as bad as any of the men who'll move heaven and earth to have you, love. I want to be inside you, your naked body under me, to feel your breasts burning against my chest, your long legs—"

"Here we are," said a cheerful voice from behind Hunter. "One Bloody Mary, one Scotch and water."

Gabby's eyes flew open, to be confronted with blazing fury and raging frustration in Hunter's. She tightened her fingers warningly and gave him a weak smile. Hunter took a deep breath and let go of her hand. He reached to release the tray on the back of the seat in front of him. "Put them both there," he ordered shortly.

He ran an impatient hand through his hair. When he caught Gabby watching him, heavy-eyed but uncertain, he gave a self-deprecating laugh. "I guess I got carried away," he said unsteadily. "I'm sorry, sweetheart. This isn't the time or the place."

Gabby blinked. She struggled to free herself from the sexual tension that was its own pressurized space. "I didn't exactly fight you off," she said in a strangely hoarse voice.

"No, you didn't, did you?" He kissed the tip of her nose very much as an elderly uncle would and settled back in his seat with a satisfied expression.

She started to give him a smart answer to the statement, but as he handed her the Bloody Mary and lifted his own drink, his fingers weren't quite steady. She looked aslant through her lashes at his face. There was the slightest film of perspiration on his brow. He had been at least as affected by the encounter as she had, she thought, and that satisfied her, too.

Just before they landed in Atlanta the captain informed them that the skies were overcast. "Are you going home today?" she asked Hunter.

"Why would I fly all the way down here if I were going home?" He seemed genuinely surprised by the question.

"Why *did* you come, Hunter? You certainly know by now that I can take care of myself."

She held her breath. If only he would say, I missed you. I wanted to be with you.

"Do I? You don't seem to realize what the consequences of your proclamation could be, Gabby," he said seriously.

"I have not made a challenge of myself," she insisted.

"Wait and see." He took the last swallow from his drink and set the empty glass on the tray beside hers. "Just wait and see." He reached for her hand again and traced the faint blue lines on her wrist with his thumb. "Besides, I missed your sharp tongue."

Well, it wasn't the same as missing *her*, but it was something of an admission from Hunter. She smiled. "Whatever the reason, I'm glad to see you."

Hunter didn't answer for a minute. When he did his grin was slightly crooked. "I'm glad to see you, too, tiger."

He was still holding her hand when they disembarked in Atlanta, to be met by a group of about ten young men holding a sign that read, Welcome, Lily Andore.

Gabby looked at Hunter, who merely shrugged and released her hand. She stepped forward to greet the welcoming party.

"Miss Andore, we're from the Northside Bachelors' Coterie. Welcome to Atlanta."

Gabby's heart sank, and she thought she heard a groan behind her. Had Hunter been right?

"We're here to escort you to your hotel."

"Thank you, but—"

The young spokesman took her arm. "And this evening you're to be our guest for dinner at the Northside Country Club. One of us will be at your disposal at all times to escort you to signings, interviews. Or, if you want to shop or do some sightseeing, we'll be more than happy to show you the best places."

"That's very nice, but don't you have to work?" she blurted out, trying to stem the flow of the young man's words.

"We've made arrangements," he said mysteriously.

The others all clustered around until Gabby found it difficult to get her breath.

"We're happy to be of service."

"We're looking forward to escorting you."

She smiled at them all uncertainly and resisted the leader's guiding hand. "Mr.—"

He slapped his forehead with a palm. "I'm sorry! I'm Deke Rogers. I guess I was so overcome...you're really a knockout, you know. Even more beautiful than your pictures." His voice lowered seductively. "I'm going to make sure you have a good time in Atlanta."

It would have taken a fool to misunderstand his meaning as he maneuvered her down the passageway with a firm grip on her arm. Frantically she glanced back over her shoulder, looking for Hunter. He was right behind her. She didn't like the self-justified gleam in his eye, but she wasn't about to argue over it now. "Mr. Rogers. Deke! I want you to meet my publisher, Hunter Graham."

Deke Rogers reluctantly released her arm to shake hands, and Gabby used the opportunity to grab onto Hunter like a lifeline. "Mr. Graham will be with me for the entire visit," she said wildly.

The young man's face fell in the presence of a man of Hunter's stamp. He was big and obviously powerful, and his mien turned every one of them into gawking schoolboys. But to give Deke Rogers's mother credit, his good manners came to the fore.

"Welcome to Atlanta, Mr. Graham. Of course, we would be delighted to have you join us for dinner, too."

Hunter inclined his head. "Thank you, Mr. Rogers. I would be delighted to accept," he answered, giving the young man back his dignity by the formal address.

Gabby's eyes thanked his warmly. It was a very nice thing to do. Still, she clung like a leech to his arm as the group of young men pelted her with questions and showered her with compliments. One man was dispatched ahead for her luggage and another to bring the car around, as the royal procession moved forward at a sedate pace.

"Virgil's law of justice: virtue is its own punishment," Hunter breathed in her ear.

"You wretch!" She grinned up at him, secure as long as she kept a hold on his arm.

The good humor between them held all the way to the hotel. Hunter even conversed pleasantly with Deke Rogers, who had insisted on driving them downtown.

The interior balconies that ringed the hotel lobby all the way to the blue dome on top of the building gave a spectacular view of the glass-enclosed elevators and the Parasol Bar with its umbrella ceiling suspended twenty stories by a slender cable. A three-piece combo near the main desk played Dixieland jazz. Hunter took care of checking in and then efficiently disentangled Gabby from the entourage with the promise that she would be ready to rejoin them at seven. They were shown to a suite on the eighteenth floor of the hotel.

While Hunter tipped the bellman, Gabby leaned out over the balcony that served in place of a hallway, delighted at the scene below. There was a mime dressed in red livery, and she tilted farther out over the balcony to get a good look at the Arab sheikh and his following who were just entering.

A hard arm came around her waist. "Careful. I'd hate to have you tumble eighteen floors."

She looked over her shoulder and smiled. "I'm sorry. It's just that this is the most interesting hotel I've been in since I started the tour."

He completed the circle with his other arm and pushed aside her hair. In the spot behind her ear, she felt his warm breath first, and then his lips. "Mmm, you smell good," he murmured.

"The hotel rooms all look—" she gasped as his teeth caught her lobe "—alike. And...." The arm beneath her breasts lifted. It was like a hot bar on the soft undercurves, sending wave after wave of heat straight up to cloud her mind. Her head fell back against his shoulder. Unconsciously her hips moved, provoking a sound from deep in his throat. "Oh, Hunter," she whispered. "I've been so lonely."

"And this is so public. I want to be alone with you, Gabby. Now." Without releasing his arms he drew her away from the barrier and walked her across the hall into the living room of the suite. One foot kicked the door shut, and then he was turning her and she was reaching for him.

Their mouths groped blindly until they met in a fevered explosion of feeling. Her arms wrapped around his neck as her mouth opened to his hot, hungry exploration. His lips were almost bruising in their urgency, as were the hands flat at the small of her back, bringing her into stunning contact with his hard arousal.

Her body flowed into the hard planes of his from the throbbing heat of his thighs to the frantic pounding of his heart against her breasts.

"There isn't time for this," he whispered hoarsely. "But I'll die if I don't see you."

She heard the rasp of her zipper and felt the cool artificiality of the air conditioning trace a path after it, all the while asking herself if she was behaving like a fool. She made no protest when he guided the silky fabric from her shoulders. Any inhibition she might have felt was erased by the warm yearning in his eyes, and the loving concern in his smile. As the dress fell in a pool around her feet, he stood back to look at her.

Hunter caught his breath at the sight of the magnificent woman before him. The French-cut bra was made of flesh-colored satin, barely covering the straining points of her nipples. It seemed to lift the fullness of her breasts in an offering to him. His eyes roamed greedily down her shape, taking in, as though it were the breath of life, the picture of the small waist defined by the elastic of her half-slip, the flat stomach and sweep of her hips, and those legs. God! Those wonderful legs! She had the body of a goddess, long and luxurious.

Her skin, caught in the light streaming through the windows behind her, was like gleaming ivory. He brought both palms up to cup her breasts from below, his fingers stroking with the lightest pressure on the bare skin above the bra where the generous roundness seemed to swell under his touch. Her skin felt as smooth and slick as the satin. He reached behind her for the fragile clasp and bared her in one motion.

Her hands fidgeted against his chest and he met her eyes. They were as dark as smoke-stained pewter, and wide with an imprecise glitter. "Don't be afraid, sweetheart. I wouldn't hurt you for anything," he vowed.

"I'm not afraid, Hunter," she whispered.

Her soft assurance was like a bomb exploding inside him. Suddenly he was yanking at his tie. His jacket fell to the floor. Half the buttons on his shirt clung just a minute too long and were ripped away.

Then he took a deep, thick breath to calm this wild impatience inside him. When he reached for her, his hands were careful on her shoulders, pulling her to him with infinite caution, as though she might take flame from his own fiery heat. He enveloped her in an embrace that was at once worshipful and erotic, moving her back and forth against his hair-roughened chest, generating a sensual friction that threatened his sanity.

Oh, dear Lord, she felt so *good* against him. A slight moan escaped his throat to become lost in the similar sound emerging from hers as their lips met in a kiss that was delicate and rich with feeling. His shoulders bent protectively over her pliant form.

With a tremendous effort at self-control he broke off the kiss, burying his face in the sweet curve of her neck. He made a purposeful effort to dampen the compelling need that burned through him like wildfire, fearing that in another second he might take her right there on the carpet. He had never wanted a woman so much in his life, wondering at the feeling, fighting it and finally surrendering. He was going to have Gabriella Constant. He was going to be the man to whom she gave herself. But not now. There wasn't time for the initiation he was planning.

His voice, when it came, was hardly recognizable. "Sweetheart, you're driving me out of my mind," he growled. "I can't work. I can't sleep. I can barely think."

In spite of the haze of desire that held Gabby in its grip, the words registered, and they bothered her somehow. Even through the labyrinth of enchanted sensation she was experiencing she knew that she didn't want to drive anyone crazy. It made her feel like some demented witch. She turned her head away in an attempt to gather her scattered reason. But the movement left the curve of her neck even more vulnerable to extended caresses.

His mouth roamed freely from the soft skin of her cheek, to her ear, to that most deliciously sensitive of all spots where neck and jaw and earlobe meet. "You didn't have to come at all, Hunter," she murmured.

"Yes. I did have to come," he said determinedly. His hand came around to hold a firm breast. "I had to. God, sweetheart, I want you!" His voice was muffled in the spill of her hair.

"Because I'm a challenge?" she inquired softly, remembering his words with a kind of hurt. Did he only want her because she looked the way she did now? What was it that was driving him crazy— these clothes designed with deliberate seduction in mind? Anyone could buy clothes.

He lifted his head, shaking it a bit to clear his vision, and finally looked with piercing honesty into her smoky eyes. The hand at her breast reluctantly left its sweet captive to circle her back.

He realized that the moment was lost, but for the life of him he couldn't figure out why. It was just as well, he thought with a sigh.

He stroked restlessly from her hips to the nape of her neck, and down again. "No, love. Because you are a warm beauty, with spirit and intelligence and the sexiest damn body I've ever held," he told her gently.

Gabby dipped her head, but he didn't let her get away with hiding her expression from him. He tilted her face with a hand beneath her chin. "What's the matter," he asked tenderly.

She ignored the small voice inside her that warned of the number of sexy bodies he had held and lifted her face to touch her lips lightly to his. "I'm not sure. I can accept the 'spirit and intelligence' part," she told him quietly. And then with a hint of a smile she added, "And I think I like the 'sexy'; but the 'beauty' still escapes me. I feel as if I'll wake up soon to find myself the way I used to be."

Hunter smoothed the tangled hair away from her face. "What you were and what you've become are the same, Gabby. The only difference in you is an awakening, not a change."

Her eyes blurred in gratitude for his insight. Her smile grew. The dynamism of this man, his sincerity and inborn worth were as much a part of him as his hands, his eyes, his mouth. "Thank you."

"There's nothing to thank me for. I still want you like hell, and I'll do anything to get you in my bed," he warned, but it was a gentle warning. "We don't have time now, but be on your guard, Lily Andore," he teased unsteadily.

Lily Andore. The name was like another dash of cold water on her sensitive and confused emotions. Lily...the writer...the center of a publicity campaign to sell books. She was saddened by the presence of Lily, despite his assurances.

"I'm tired, Hunter. I think I'd like to rest for a few minutes."

Hunter took a breath and let it out slowly. He pressed his lips to her forehead. Tonight, he thought. Tonight when they were alone, with no deadline to meet, no dinner engagement.... He could wait. "Okay, sweetheart. I have some calls to make." He kept his tone deliberately neutral.

Little did he know that the casual tone, the controlled features, only reinforced Gabby's misgivings.

What had she done, she asked herself. Gone into his arms as though she belonged there, answered his kisses as though she alone had experienced them. She grabbed for her dress and, holding it in front of her, backed away from him until his words halted her.

"We don't have to be downstairs until seven." He consulted his watch. "That gives you almost an hour. Can you be ready?"

She gave him a small salute. "Ready and waiting, sir."

GABBY SURVEYED HERSELF in the full-length mirror. The black dress was indecent, no doubt about it. It was one of the ones she had tried on that first day in Betsy Powers's boutique. That one brief experience hadn't been long enough to show her the dangers of the dress. It was fine as long as she didn't move a muscle—or breathe.

She delved into her bag and came up with a roll of masking tape. Carefully she tore off a piece and folded it across her fingers, making a circle with the sticky side out. Placed strategically along the inner curve of her breast, the tape held the dress securely in place. She repeated the process on the other side and looked again, then took a huge deep breath and swung her arms wildly. So far so good. She leaned over and twisted her body from side to side before she was finally satisfied.

Gabby chuckled as she remembered the first time she had worn the dress. Old-fashioned cellophane tape was the only kind available in the hotel shop, but she'd sailed forth to the television studio for a late-night interview confident that no one would see more of her than she intended. Unfortunately the heat of the lights and the resulting perspiration on her body had caused the cellophane tape to curl up and die after the first five minutes. She had sat with rigid posture and a stiff smile for the rest of the hour.

She laughed aloud, remembering. That was in Chicago. Or was it San Francisco? The cities were all alike when all you were able to see of them were hotel rooms, studios and shopping malls.

A knock on her bedroom door startled her. "You're early," she said as she swung open the door and turned back to the room. "Just let me put on my shoes." She missed the black frown that crossed Hunter's brow.

"Where the hell did you get that dress?" he grated.

She looked up in surprise from her bent-over position as she worked with the tiny buckles and straps. His eyes were riveted to the bare skin between the sides of the dress.

Fighting the urge to put up a concealing hand, she kept her voice steady. After all, she *was* taped in securely. "This is Lily Andore's dress. You selected it," she told him.

"*I* did?" He gave disbelieving snort. "I don't remember it. I'm sure I would remember a dress like that."

Gabby was amazed at the childish petulance in his voice. Her fingers fumbled at their task. Finally she had the straps fastened and she straightened in relief. The high heels still didn't bring her anywhere near his height, but they helped when she had to deal with his intimidating presence. He looked so disturbingly masculine and assured in evening clothes.

"Shall we go?" she asked blithely, picking up the tiny beaded evening bag from the dresser.

He eyed her with distrust. "Are you sure you won't come out of that dress?"

"I'm sure," she stated flatly, and headed for the door, leaving Hunter to trail along after her with his hands thrust into the pockets of his tuxedo pants. He still wore the sulky glare of a spoiled boy.

HUNTER WATCHED HER dance and flirt, and his scowl grew blacker as the evening wore on. The club they had been taken to had an orchestra, and after dinner the entire group, which had grown considerably since the airport, moved into the dimly lit lounge. Gabby moved from one partner to another, but she didn't dance with anyone a second time. She kept one eye on Hunter, hoping he would cut in, but he seemed in no mood to dance.

Finally, she decided, it was time to go. "I've really enjoyed the evening, Deke, but I have to be up early tomorrow." She smiled at the patent disappointment in the faces around her. They were really very nice boys.

A deep voice interrupted their protests. "I think that's an excellent idea," said Hunter. "Would you call us a taxi, Mr. Rogers. There's really no reason for you to drive all the way back downtown."

"I don't mind at all, Mr. Graham."

"Nevertheless, we'll take a cab," Hunter informed him in a voice that warned against argument.

All the way up in the glass elevator, Gabby watched the muscle in Hunter's jaw with fascination. It throbbed like a tiny heartbeat. Despite his easy charm with their hosts, the muscle betrayed his annoyance.

The heavy doors slid back, and he motioned politely for her to precede him. Hunter was never merely polite! She walked in front of him around the balcony to the door of the suite and waited while he unlocked it. She scooted through, but before she could escape to her room she was brought up short by his hand on her arm. He kicked the door shut and whirled her around until her back was against the panels. Her hands came up to his chest in an automatic move to hold him off.

He took her purse and tossed it onto a table without ever releasing his hold.

"You really enjoy the femme fatale role, don't you? You enjoy being Lily," he growled.

"Don't be silly." She squirmed, trying to release herself, and he retaliated by pinning her hips to the door with his own. The thrust of hard muscle against soft curves was a shock, and she ceased all movement immediately, watching him with wide, wary eyes.

"Oh, yes," he said unpleasantly. "You've never had so much masculine attention and you loved having all those men panting in their soup. You've developed the habit of twisting men around your finger very quickly, haven't you? What would your mother say if she could see how her daughter has turned into a Sadie Thompson?"

She tried to hit him then, withdrawing one hand to aim for the side of his head. But they were standing too close for the blow to have any force—if it had landed. He caught her wrist effortlessly and held it against the door beside her head.

"You bastard! Let me go."

"First, let's see how you handle the real thing. Those boys don't have enough experience to satisfy you. I, on the other hand, have had a lot of experience." His voice took on a thick huskiness. His other hand threaded into her hair to hold her head immobile while his mouth descended slowly and relentlessly toward her own.

She expected a crushing kiss, given in anger, but what she received was a gentle but sensuous assault on her reason. He took tender, moist bites of her lips, his tongue coaxing, tempting her to part them. The scent of him added its urging—a subtle after-shave mingled with fine tobacco, expensive Scotch and the clean male essense of his skin. Finally his deep, throaty voice joined the onslaught of persuasion.

"Open your mouth, Gabriella," he murmured.

Perhaps it was the shock of hearing her full name on his lips. No one except her mother had ever called her Gabriella, not within the limits of her memory, and the sound of it in slightly thickened tones stirred something in her that she wanted to feel again. Her sound judgment took a holiday. She melted against him, her parted lips granting him the access he sought, and gave herself up to the excitement of his kiss, with none of the reservations of the afternoon.

And then suddenly she was free.

"I'm going down to the lounge for a drink," Hunter informed her. He took the key from his pocket, tossed it in the air and caught it with a side swipe. "Good night."

Gabby stood staring at him with a stunned expression that brought out one last smile before he walked through the door and closed it very softly behind him. He'd left her!

How long she stood staring at the door she didn't

know, but suddenly she made a decision. She grabbed her purse and opened the door.

Fifteen minutes later she was descending an escalator to a second level beneath the main lobby and trying to count the number of lounges in this hotel. She had been to the crown of the building, back down to the lobby, up the steps to the suspended bar and down the escalator, and as far as she could discover this one on the second level was her last hope. She heard music and stepped off the escalator to approach a dark cavern of a room.

"May I help you?" A lovely hostess in a silver sequined dress smiled from the door.

"I'm looking for someone," Gabby told her. "But I may never find him in this light." She peered around.

"You're welcome to look. Why don't you come in and let your eyes adjust."

Gabby stepped inside. Candlelit tables were grouped around a crowded dance floor. A five-man combo provided the music, a soft ballad, and couples swayed to the rhythm. She watched them, remembering how it had felt to be in Hunter's arms.

"Would you like to dance?" said the deep voice at her elbow.

Slowly she turned to look up at him. Her full lips curved into a relieved smile. "Yes, Hunter. Yes, I would like that very much," she breathed.

His arm circled her back to fit her closely against him. He curved their clasped hands into his chest, and she felt him let out a deep breath. "I didn't think you were coming," he said into her hair.

It was heaven. Gabby let her head fall to his shoulder, her lips just brushing the skin under his chin. "I've been looking everywhere for you," she heard herself say.

"Have you, tiger?" His low voice vibrated the air next to her ear.

"Were you jealous, Hunter?" She was surprised at her own daring.

His lips feathered across her cheek, and he gave a low chuckle. "I guess I was," he admitted.

She leaned back to look at him with a teasing smile. "Of those boys? You ought to know that none of them could compete with you."

He looked into her eyes. He was trying to read in them what her true feelings were, but she kept her expression playful. "You're always walking out on me."

Her lips formed a delicious pout that he couldn't resist. His arm drew her closer again. "Come back here." He bent his head to kiss her softly. "You've learned a lot in a short time," he murmured.

"And most of it you've taught me," she agreed.

"Gabriella." Her name on his lips produced the same sensual quiver that she'd experienced in the room upstairs. "There are other things I want to teach you. Will you let me?"

"I—I don't know, Hunter."

They were still moving to the music, but Gabby knew that if the music stopped, the momentum of their own rhythm would continue. The experience of the moment was like a staircase, and she had taken the next step toward the unknown. Was she prepared to climb to the top with him?

A small gasp escaped against his neck as she felt an exploring finger at the exposed hollow between her breasts. It moved slowly, with only the slightest touch, to trace the curve, before sliding inside the fabric. Wherever it touched it left a ribbon of heat. The finger delved farther into the darkness between them and came in contact with something that shouldn't have been there. Slowly it withdrew and he lifted his head to peer down at her in the dim light. "Gabriella, what is that?" he asked mildly.

She chuckled. "That's masking tape. To keep me from coming out of this dress."

Suddenly both arms were around her. Hunter laughed helplessly into the soft skin of her neck. "I wish you'd told me it was there earlier. I wouldn't have worried so much."

Gabby was hardly listening. The strong arms enfolding her had brought her into closer contact with the heat of his body. The effect was weakening her bones, sending her heart on a racing ride. "Hunter, if you don't want me to embarrass you by collapsing at your feet, we'd better get out of here," she warned breathlessly.

"You want me, too," he whispered triumphantly.

"Well-l-l," she hedged. "Yes, but that doesn't mean that I . . . that we will . . . ."

"Let's go." He kept a supporting arm around her and walked her to the door.

The escalator looked like a mountain, but eventually it took them to the level of the lobby. There they had to wait for the elevator. Gabby looked toward the ceiling twenty stories up and watched as the brightly lit cage descended. It seemed to take an interminable time, stopping at almost every floor. She couldn't control the sigh of impatience that escaped her.

"It won't be long now, sweetheart."

Gabby stood up straight with an effort. What was she doing? Hunter seemed quite sure that they were going to make love. She finally found her voice. "I don't think I'm ready for this," she told him. "This kind of decision should be thought out very carefully."

The doors opened and he led her inside the empty elevator. "I didn't ask you to make the decision. Haven't you ever heard of Homer's law of practicality?" The car began its quick rise and this time there were no stops along the way.

"No-o-o," she said suspiciously. They were outside the door to the suite. Hunter reached for the key, but he didn't answer until they were inside and the chain was in place. Then he swung her easily up into his arms. The black sandals hit the floor. He crossed to her darkened bedroom.

"Forgiveness is easier to obtain than permission," he said as he gently set her on her feet beside the bed.

8

"Now, Hunter, wait just a minute." Gabby couldn't keep the smile from her lips.

"Okay." Hunter folded his arms across his broad chest and stepped back.

"Okay?" Gabby said weakly. Wasn't he going to try to overcome her objections? She took a half step toward him, looking up in puzzlement. They seemed to be at some sort of impasse, and she wasn't sure what to do next.

He nodded, looking very serious.

A tiny frown appeared between her brows. "Hunter, please...."

"Please, what, Gabriella?"

Suddenly she understood. Despite his teasing he wasn't going to force her. She had to want him as much as he wanted her. The game they'd been playing was almost over.

She was a woman. This man had guided her from girlish inexperience to maturity, brought her full sensuality to the surface, but he'd never let her flounder. All the while he'd stood securely behind her, waiting until the moment was right, until *she* was ready. He'd flown to Philadelphia, to New Orleans, to be there in case she needed him. That was caring beyond a feeling of responsibility or a concern for book sales, wasn't it?

It was time to put aside her unwillingness to be judged against the glamorous, sophisticated women he had known, to put aside her doubts about her own worth. She had always had faith in herself, trust in her abilities and instincts. It was only with the creation of Lily Andore that she'd begun to question her worth, and then only on a physical level. That was over. She was ready to take the final step out of her safe but lonely world.

She took the step, albeit tentatively, toward Hunter. "Please make love with me," she said softly.

Slowly his arms unfolded. "Are you sure?"

Gabby planted her hands on her hips in mock exasperation and smiled a lovely smile. "Well," she drawled. "I thought I was, but if you're going to procrastinate...."

Her words were lost in his kiss as she was swept against him. His hands came up to tangle in her hair, cupping her head, his lips melting into hers.

Gabby slid her arms around his waist under his jacket to cling to the soft folds of his silk shirt while she gave herself up completely to the joy of his hungry embrace.

He drew back to breathe, then he was covering her face with kisses, murmuring her name in a voice choked with desire. She twisted her head, seeking his lips, and gave a soft little cry. "Hunter!"

A deep shudder shook his large frame, and he wrapped his arms about her, rocking her slightly. "Shh, sweetheart. Wait a minute." His voice held an unexpectedly desperate note.

She subsided, letting him take the lead. He knew where they were going; she didn't, but she trusted him to guide her along the pathways of love.

Finally Hunter lifted his head to look down at her with a tender smile. He brushed back a strand of hair from her moist lips with a hand that shook slightly. A thumb stayed to outline her mouth. "It isn't fair for one woman to be so exciting."

"You are, too," she murmured, her eyes dazed with arousal.

He ignored her remark. "But we're going to take it very slowly, Gabriella." He nudged her away just far enough for his hand to slide between them. He found the tape on one breast and gently stripped it away, but despite his care she couldn't hide a little wince. He moved the dress aside until it barely covered her nipple. "Oh, sweetheart, your beautiful skin!" he groaned. His lips found the reddened spot, tenderly drawing out the sting of pain with their touch.

Tingles of warmth spread from his mouth over her body, sending the blood singing through her veins. She cradled his head closer, her fingers threading through his black hair. He repeated the operation with the other piece of tape and then slowly, with almost torturous deliberation, he pulled the sides of the dress back until her rosy-tipped breasts were exposed completely. The intensity of his burning gaze threatened to collapse her knees.

"This is what I've wanted to do all night. To unwrap you like a Christmas present," he said in a husky voice as his broad hands came up to take the weight of her full breasts. His fingers scraped lightly over the sensitive nipples, sending them into hardening shock, and his palms began a tender massage. Each movement had the effect of slow motion, dragging out the excitement until it stretched to blissful torture.

Gabby's head fell back as a throbbing began in the lower part of her body. She swayed on her feet in a confusion of passionate longing.

Hunter sensed her reaction, and lifting her easily he set her on the bed. Reaching beneath her he slid the zipper of the dress down and languidly stripped the flimsy garment away, leaving her clad in only the briefest of panties and sheerest of hose.

All at once Gabby was impatient to see him, too. She slanted a look up at him and whispered weakly, "I know that this is an important event, but must you be dressed so formally, Hunter?"

He chuckled and stood to shrug out of his jacket. Gabby followed, getting to her knees at the edge of the bed. She tugged at his black tie and began to work on the buttons of his shirt. He stood quiet under her hands for a moment, but she could feel his big body tremble with the effort.

She met his eyes and shyness overcame her. Her hands faltered and his came out to clamp on her shoulders, his eyes shining with a yearning that beseeched her to continue even before he spoke. "Don't stop!" he rasped. "Don't you know I ache to feel your hands on me?"

Emboldened by the sudden new power she had acquired, Gabby curved her lips into a seductive smile. She caught her lower lip between white even teeth and pushed back the shirt to bare his massive chest. Her fingers moved slowly across the muscular expanse, tangling in the wiry hair. "You feel warm," she whispered. Her nails made tiny trails across his skin until they reached his hard nipples.

He inhaled sharply. His eyes drifted shut. "Warm?" he laughingly groaned. "God! I'm burning." His hands dropped to her hips, drawing her against him until she felt the hard force of his desire.

Slowly her hands stroked up to his shoulders and wound sensuously around his neck. She pressed closer, reveling in the slight abrasion of his wiry hair on her breasts.

The movement seemed to send him over the edge. A deep husky growl escaped from his throat and he followed her down onto the mattress, covering her slenderness from shoulder to toe with his large strong body. His mouth was moist with its greed to taste the warmth and the sweetness beyond her lips.

Gabby twisted her hands in his hair, bringing him farther into her. Her tongue joined in the slow, sensuous exploration. A moment of chilling separation forced a whimper from her throat. He quelled it with a tender kiss on her midriff just below her throbbing breast as he divested them of their remaining clothes. Seconds later she felt the weight of an unclad body against her nakedness for the first time.

She hesitated, not really from fear...except, perhaps, fear of the unknown. "That feels...."

He sensed her anxiety even before he heard the uneasiness in her voice. "Easy, darling." His hands gentled on her body, stroking with caresses that were once again controlled, until he felt the trembling subside. Then he began to stoke the fires again, and they flamed rapidly into a consuming inferno.

Gabby took a long breath. "I'm sorry to be such a baby," she gasped against his shoulder.

"I'm not sorry. God! I'm no better than any of those panting boys. I'm glad you're untouched! Don't you know that?" His broad hand covered her stomach, sliding down to urge her legs apart. The words were ground out against the stiff peak of her breast.

She arched with a convulsive movement. "I'm glad, too! I'm glad that it's you! Oh, Hunter," she cried softly. "Please...."

Tenderly he found the back of her knee with one hand and lifted it, sliding his large body into the cradle of her femininity, poised for the gentle thrust that would carry her to heights of pleasure she'd never known.

Gabby could never have described or explained, or understood, without having had experienced. The anticipation, the expansion...and suddenly there was a whole new universe within the confines of her body and her heart, a climbing pleasure-laden clarification of the length and breadth and width of consciousness, of awareness.

The fires built, feeding on themselves, as she twisted and writhed beneath him, wildly, mindlessly, the only reality that of a man joined with a woman in the timeless union of two souls soaring together.

Other infinite regions were reached with a suddenness that stopped her heartbeat, regions illuminated by the light of the blaze as it exploded into millions of burning comets shooting across the stardappled heavens.

"Look at me," he ordered huskily after a minute.

Her lids felt heavy. She wasn't sure she could lift them, but her lips curved into a delicious, satiated smile. Finally she peeked through the long lashes to meet his eyes. The expression there, so tender, so loving, almost took her breath away.

What he read in hers must have satisfied him, for he covered her lips with a final, exquisitely gentle kiss. "You're beautiful," he sighed, easing his weight from her but not breaking the circle of his arms.

Her head nestled into the haven between his shoulder and his chest. On impulse she tasted the salty flavor of his skin. "So are you," she whispered.

"Sleep now, love."

GABBY ALWAYS AWAKENED INSTANTLY, clearheaded and bright as soon as she opened her eyes. Five inches from her face was another, and she only had to blink once to adjust to this unfamiliar situation. They lay on their sides. Her hand rested lightly over his heart. His arm was at her waist, his broad hand established possessively on the small of her back.

Hunter looked young, and relaxed, and devastatingly handsome. This was an unexpected luxury, to be able to look and examine every feature to her heart's content. The unruly black hair had fallen forward over his brow. She wanted to brush it back, to run her fingers into its thickness, but not yet. The lashes on his cheeks were thick and black, but she found one gray hair in his left brow. Her eyes traveled down the aristocratic nose to his mouth, and at the memory of all the things it could do she blushed hotly. As she watched the lips curved into a smile.

"Am I forgiven?" he whispered.

She had to think for a minute. Then her brow cleared and she smiled. "You did it the hard way; you got permission first."

The muscles under her hand began to stir like a giant slowly awakening, and she felt the chuckle grow to a deep husky laugh as his eyes finally opened. Suddenly she was flipped onto her back and penned by his body. His weight rested on his forearms with his hands tangled in her hair. The glow in his eyes held amusement and the reawakening of desire.

Gabby's heart swelled into her throat. She lifted a hand to his cheek, rubbing a palm along the bristly growth of his beard.

He dipped his head to taste the hollow in her throat and strung a necklace of kisses up to the sensitive spot just below her ear. "Are you hungry?"

Gabby arched her neck to give him more room for his exploration. "What time is it?" Her hands roamed restlessly over his back. She could feel the muscles bunch under her fingers.

"Early."

"I would love some coffee," she murmured.

"The phone's on your side. Why don't you order us some?" His lips hovered over hers. His warm breath filled her mouth, but he skimmed with a light touch of his tongue over her lower lip, making her ache for more.

Gabby stretched out a hand, fumbling for the telephone, and managed to knock the receiver to the floor. She moaned and closed her eyes, lifting her arms to wrap them around his neck. "Who wanted coffee anyway?" she gasped. "That was a terrible idea."

The hands in her hair tilted her head slightly to more fully receive the force of his kiss. His tongue plunged in to probe and explore anew every secret of her mouth. "Oh, God, Gabriella, you taste so damned sweet," he groaned into her mouth. "Like warm honey. Like champagne and peaches."

She curved around him, accepting his hard body against her softer feminine curves. "Then why not have me for breakfast?" she teased seductively.

Hunter lifted his head to peer down at her with a hungry grin. "You learn fast, don't you?" He seemed to be delighted at the discovery.

Her eyes darkened seriously. "I think the credit should go to you."

A bolt of pure gold flashed from the dark eyes, warming her to her toes. He began her second lesson.

AGAIN GABBY WOKE FIRST with a wonderful feeling of complete happiness. She slid out from under the arm that held her in a light embrace and stumbled slightly on the way to the bathroom.

The hot shower eased some of the pleasurable ache. She stood for a long time, letting the warm water pelt and soothe her body.

When she came out wrapped in a thick terry-cloth robe, her wet hair twisted into a coil on top of her head, Hunter was still asleep. He was sprawled atop her pillow, one sinewy arm cradling it to his face.

She smiled and blew him a silent kiss. After quietly putting the bedside phone back on the hook, she tiptoed to the living room. There she closed the door carefully and crossed to the telephone, intent on ordering coffee.

While she waited for room service Gabby hugged herself and looked out over a bright, sun-soaked Peachtree Street. She felt like a different person today. How extraordinary! The idea was hackneyed and had always seemed silly to her. Even after the abrupt change in her life-style that the book had brought about, she'd never felt like a different person, just someone who looked different on the outside. She had been propelled into an unfamiliar world, but she was still the same Gabby Constant inside.

This change, however, was bone deep, soul deep. She was a blossom opening its delicate new petals for the first touch of sunlight, swelling and spreading to absorb and reflect its vibrant living color in the warmth.

Hunter was the sun. What a romantic thought, she marveled.

All at once she whirled, her eyes searching the room for her briefcase. Words of love and passion spilled from her heart. One way or another they demanded release. She couldn't say them out loud—not now, not yet, maybe not ever to Hunter—but she could write them. She didn't know how he really felt about her, whether it was affection and desire that would blaze fiercely and die quickly, or an emotion to match hers, one that she knew instinctively would burn forever in her heart even if she never saw him again.

She had filled two pages of foolscap when the waiter finally knocked at the door. So lost in her thoughts was she that she looked at the man blankly for a moment before waving him in. What time was it? She was supposed to be at the bookstore at nine-thirty. Her watch was in the bedroom, but the man supplied the time along with a morning paper.

"It's seven-thirty, ma'am."

"And how long will it take me to get to Lenox Square Mall?" she asked.

"Only about twenty minutes."

Gabby breathed a sigh of relief. She wouldn't be late, but on the other hand there was no time to waste, either. She poured two cups of coffee and went back to the bedroom. One she placed on the table beside the bed with a cheerful, "Good morning," and the other she took with her to the dresser across the room.

She snapped open the small dressing case and reached for a jar of moisturizer. As she began the morning ritual she watched in the mirror as Hunter slowly stirred, rolled over and reached for the coffee.

His broad shoulders settled against the pillows comfortably. The sheet fell to his waist, exposing the generous growth of hair across his chest. He met her eyes in the mirror as he raised the cup in silent salute.

As she smoothed a light foundation over her skin, Gabby's dimple deepened. She accepted the unspoken communication with immediate perception. He must be one of those people who don't want to talk in the mornings. Her mother was like that, so she was accustomed to silence over coffee.

His eyes followed each movement. It was strange that she didn't feel self-conscious under his warm gaze, almost as though she'd done this every morning of her life.

The application of mascara took all of her concentration. She leaned forward, stroking the tiny brush upward over her already thick lashes.

Unnoticed Hunter came up behind her to wrap his arms around her waist.

Gabby jumped at the sudden warm sensation, smearing black across her cheek. "Oh, damn!" she murmured weakly. "Look what you made me do."

She grabbed for a tissue, but gently Hunter turned her to face him and took it out of her hand. She was surprised that she wasn't shy about being confronted with his nudity. His body was superbly proportioned, like a living, breathing sculpture. It seemed the most natural thing in the world to be standing next to him with only her robe separating them.

He wiped away the smear carefully and peered down into her upturned face. "You don't need all that goop anyway."

Her jaw dropped. She shook her head and began to laugh softly. "You're the one who said I did!"

He folded her into his arms, resting his cheek against her temple to rock them slowly with a gentle rhythm. It was lovely, being held like this.

"I know," he murmured. "But it wasn't the makeup, or the clothes, or the hairstyle. You just looked so damn young!"

"I *was* young," she agreed. "I was an infant compared to the women you were used to." Her brows furrowed. She didn't like to think about those women.

Hunter tilted up her chin with a broad hand. He examined her face slowly, taking in every feature, lingering longest on her lips, which were pink and moist. "You don't look like an infant any longer," he whispered. His kiss was as devastating in the morning as it was at night, she thought fleetingly, before succumbing to the potency of it.

AN HOUR LATER Gabby sat at the small table in the living room of the suite, finishing the notes she'd started earlier while she waited for Hunter. The words of description flowed from her pen with an ease she'd never dreamed possible when she was writing *Captive of Her Bed*. The reactions of her body had been at once languorous and greedy, generous and demanding, and she had an idea that Valentine Semmes would have enjoyed her amorous adventures so much more if she had known Hunter Graham.

Gabby lifted her head to stare with half-closed eyes toward the blue sky beyond the window. A smile of feminine satisfaction curved her lips while the pen dipped a dimple into her cheek. She felt his presence before he spoke—a warmth at her back, a flattened palm on the table beside her notes. She started to lean back in her chair, instinctively moving toward the warm contact that her body wanted.

He nuzzled her neck. "Mmm. You look good enough to take a bite of."

She had chosen the same red silk shirtwaist dress that she'd worn for that first morning show in New York. It was one of her favorite outfits, the bright color giving her spirits a boost on the most harrowing day. Suddenly her eyes flew open. Her notes! She slapped her hands down on the papers, but that was the wrong thing to do.

"What's this?" Hunter asked as he pulled the sheets free.

She grabbed for them. "Nothing."

He moved a step away, lifting them beyond her reach.

"Hunter, please! Those are private!" She pleaded with him to no avail. As she watched, his eyes skimmed over her words. His features took on the hard angry cast that she knew so well and had hoped never to see again.

"What the hell is this, Gabby?" He didn't raise his voice, he didn't shout. Instead he looked down at where she still sat with an icy cold glare, and posed another perfectly controlled question. "Have I been used for research?"

"Of course not, Hunter," she answered, but her profound embarrassment at this unexpected exposure made her voice less firm than she would have wished.

He tossed the sheets onto the table with too much unconcern and pushed back the cuff of his white shirt to look at his watch. "We'd better go," he said. "Your escort is probably blocking the entrance to the hotel right now. I'm leaving on the afternoon flight. Perhaps one or more of your new *boy*friends could provide further research." He sounded as though the thought didn't disturb him in the least.

"Hunter!" she let out on a breath. The pain was unbelievable. She touched his forearm and raised wide smoky eyes to his. "You don't really mean that, do you?" she asked softly. "It didn't...I don't...."

He shook off her hand, but only to pull her hard into his arms. "Hell, no! You know I don't mean it," he groaned into her hair. "Why do you do such crazy things? Make me say such crazy things? Taking *notes*, for God's sake!" He broke off with a husky chuckle. "You're impossible!"

She curled closer against him. "I'm sorry, Hunter," she murmured. "I just felt so many things, so much...." She shook her head against his hand. "I wanted to sing or something."

He tilted her face up with a broad hand. "Sing?" The brow with the gray hair quirked.

"But I can't carry a tune."

He laughed and gave her a brief but tender kiss. "Do you think you could manage to stay out of trouble until Washington?"

The American Booksellers' Association was holding its annual convention there the next week. Gabby had two more stops on her tour, Miami and Charleston, before winding up at the convention. "I'll try," she promised with a relieved smile, but she wondered... was that a hint of doubt she still read in his eyes?

He let her go with a peck on the nose. "Get your purse. We don't want to keep the autograph hounds waiting."

When she reentered the room a minute later, Hunter had donned the jacket to his dark suit and was holding the sheets again.

Gabby caught her breath, then said calmly, "I'm ready if you are." She began to move toward the door.

His gaze swung to her. There was something unusual in his taciturn expression—a hint of confusion in his reserve, hesitation in his silence. Finally he spoke. "Did I really make you feel like that?" he asked softly.

Her footsteps faltered. What did he expect her to say? She looked away. "You don't ask much, do you?" Her voice sounded dry, hollow.

The sound of his laughter surprised her into meeting his glowing gaze. The vigor was there, the vibrant power and bold, self-assured masculinity. As he reached in front of her for the knob, his other hand settled at her waist. He bent down to leave a kiss on the curve of her neck.

"You pleased me, too, tiger," he said against her skin. "More than I could ever describe on paper."

9

THE LARGE CROWD that had waited at Atlanta's largest shopping mall to meet Lily Andore merited a mention on the noonday news.

Hunter was in the second bedroom, packing to leave.

Gabby sat on the deep sofa with her stocking feet propped on the table in front of her, munching on a sandwich and listening to the sounds of an off-key whistle from his bedroom. She made a face at herself on the television. Simpering idiot, she called the TV image. She might have learned to cope with the media, but she would never be comfortable and at ease in front of a camera, and it showed.

She glanced at her watch. It was almost time for Hunter to leave, and she still hadn't made a decision. She thought of the package in the bottom of her suitcase. It had been waiting to be delivered to her in Dallas, and she'd carried it ever since. Finally she set her sandwich on the plate and wiped her lips with a decisive swipe of the white linen napkin. "Hunter, I have a present for you," she called out as she stood and padded into her bedroom.

He appeared in the doorway while she was still rummaging in the bottom of her suitcase. "A present?" he asked, raising a quizzical brow.

"I hope you're going to like it," she told him as

she pulled out the large manila envelope. "It's my new book." She turned, offering the package to him, but instead of taking it he let out a whoop and wrapped his arms around her to lift her clear off the floor.

"Wonderful! I didn't know you'd been working on another one!" He gave her an enthusiastic kiss before letting her slide down until her feet touched the floor.

"Hunter, I think I ought to warn you. It isn't like the other book."

He took the manuscript, not even glancing at it, and dropped it on top of her opened suitcase. His arm came back around her. "I should hope not," he murmured against her lips.

"And I haven't been...able to come up with a title. Maybe...maybe you can suggest something," she whispered breathlessly between his kisses.

The telephone rang. "Damn! That's probably my driver," he complained, releasing her to cross to the phone. A sales representative for the publishing house had offered to drive him to the airport. After a brief conversation he came back to enfold her in a hungry embrace. "I hate to leave you," he said seriously in his husky baritone.

Gabby leaned back in his arms, cradling his face in her white hands. The contrast between her skin and his tanned face was startling. Her fingers roamed, enjoying the feel of his skin, the slight roughness where his beard would grow and shadow his face by tonight. She already knew that he had to shave twice a day. She knew so many things about him—that he was an exquisitely tender lover, that though he had a short temper he got over his anger quickly. Occasionally, however, he would show patience when she most expected him to explode.

Hunter turned his face into her hand, nuzzling her palm. "I'll miss you, tiger."

"I'll miss you, too," she admitted softly, raising herself on tiptoe until their lips were on a level, their breath mingling in sweet temptation. Her mouth brushed his, tantalizing, and she smiled. "Kiss me goodbye." The order was given in a sweetly seductive whisper.

He made a frustrated sound deep in his throat and complied, with all the hunger of a man who knows he will starve for a week. His hands moved restlessly up and down her back from hip to shoulder, rustling the red silk. "I've got to go," he growled unsteadily, but made no move to release her. Then suddenly his fingers tangled in the mass of her hair and he was covering her face with stinging kisses, stopping at her slightly swollen lips. "I'll call you," he rasped, and picking up the manuscript he was gone.

Gabby stood where she was until she heard the outer door of the suite close quietly. At the sound all the self-control that held her together seemed to escape with her long sigh. She sank to sit cross-legged on the plush carpet and stared blindly through the open door into the living room.

She was in love with the Great Hunter Graham. Oceans, caverns deep, mountains, sky high, in love. Her eyes fell shut, her lips parted. She ran her fingertips slowly, lightly across their outline and smiled, a silly little grin. She chuckled, and the sound in the quiet room startled her eyes open again. Energy began to return to her limbs. She wanted to shout, to dance, to throw back her head and laugh like a loon.

Rising in one swift movement, she made a circuit of the rooms on quick feet, touching a chair where he'd sat, sipping from his glass of iced tea on the luncheon tray. In the other bedroom, the one he had used only to dress, she ran her fingers across the mirror that had held his image. She felt crazy, insane and wildly, unbelievably happy.

Her restless movement slowed to a saunter. Being in love with the Great Hunter Graham was going to pose some definite problems, not the least of which was her new manuscript. Her warning that it was different had been an understatement. Would he like it? It was certainly a more ambitious work than *Captive*. She'd begun the research in college, when collecting information about turn-of-the-century America had become a hobby with her. It wasn't the most exciting period, but she loved ferreting out bits of information about these comparatively placid years of American history.

She shrugged, impatient with herself for building obstacles where there were none. Of course he would like it. He cared for her. He would be proud that she'd attempted a history of the period. Still, at the thought of Hunter reading her words, turning the loose pages one by one, her palms became moist. She had mailed *Captive* as a lark and promptly forgotten it, but this book meant more to her. With this one she would wait in trepidation for a verdict. With this one she would bury Lily Andore at least for the present, though someday she might want to finish the sequel she had started.

If only he could have stayed, if she could have watched his expression as he read. She smiled, doubting seriously that he would be reading if he were here, and doubting also that she would be watching his expression.

She should find something to do to fill the empty hours of the afternoon and evening before the ten o'clock flight to Miami the next morning. Flipping on the television, she twisted the dial to run the gamut of channels, then flipped it off again. It had taken such a short time for the loneliness to return, such a very short time. She walked, still in stocking feet, to the bedroom they had shared.

The quilted spread was now smooth, thanks to an invisible housekeeper, and his towel had been taken away along with hers. She stretched out across the bed and reached for the pillow. The sheets were fresh. *They didn't even leave me his pillowcase*, she thought sadly, and drifted off to sleep hugging the sterile white bolster.

WHEN GABBY HEARD THE BELL she struggled to rise from the depths of sleep. Disoriented in the dark, she looked around in frantic confusion. The only light was the dial of the clock on the bedside table, but it was familiar enough to quiet the pounding of her heart. Nine o'clock. She fumbled for the lamp switch before picking up the telephone receiver.

"H-hello." The word came out as a hoarse whisper, so she cleared her throat and tried again. "Hello?"

A husky chuckle preceded Hunter's greeting. "Hello, tiger. You must have gone to sleep early."

She slid up on the bed and pushed the pillow behind her shoulder. "Is it nine o'clock?" She gave a huge yawn. "I was only going to have a short nap." Looking at the crumpled red silk in disgust, she added without thinking, "I must have been more tired than I thought."

To give him credit he didn't gloat. "What are you planning for dinner?" he asked almost too casually.

She yawned again. "Umm. I don't know, I hadn't thought about it," she mused lazily.

"You need to eat."

She grinned. "I suppose I could call Deke."

"Gabriella...." His voice took on a warning note.

"Well, what would you suggest?" she asked innocently.

"How about room service?" he offered gruffly.

She grinned at the telephone. He was jealous! "That's a wonderful idea, Hunter. I can watch the X-rated movie channel while I eat, since I don't have you for research."

Hunter gave a reluctant laugh. "Am I supposed to be pleased with that comparison?"

Gabby's eyes widened in surprise. She had been teasing, but he was still irritated over the scene that morning. She wasn't sure how to reassure him without giving away her own newly tender feelings, so she was less than honest for the first time. She forced a laugh, thinking wryly that she was learning fast to play the game of sophisticated repartee.

"You've introduced me into a whole new world, Hunter," she told him grandly. "Who knows where my research will take me? By the way, did you read any of the new manuscript?"

There was a silence on the other end of the line. "I had some other work with me," he answered ambiguously. "Has Nina seen it?"

"No. I have a copy for her here, but I haven't mailed it yet."

"Don't bother. I'll send a copy over to her," he said roughly.

The sharp tones stung her. Hunter's end of the conversation was deteriorating rapidly into something she didn't understand—from light teasing to definite chill. The tension was coming across the wires like an October fog on the Hudson River, and it crept into her bones, leaving her feeling strangely vulnerable and frightened by his remoteness. "Is there anything wrong, Hunter?"

"Should there be?" There it was again, that harshness.

She didn't understand, but the telephone wasn't the best place to try. If only she could see him. She swallowed. "Well, I guess I'll see you in Washington," she said faintly.

"I'll be there to meet your plane."

"Oh, but...." She was arriving a day early, before the convention even started. Did he want a day alone with her? A smile began on her face. "Is mother coming, too?" she asked to cover the leap her heart took.

"No, she'll come with Daphne. I thought we'd have a day alone together. You might be ready for some more research by then." His attitude brought their lovemaking down to a level that was almost vulgar.

Gabby didn't, couldn't, answer. She blinked the sudden moisture from her eyes. How could he lift her heart so, only to dash it down with a cruel statement like that? "Hunter, what's wrong?"

She hadn't considered her virginity a precious gift—not when she was twenty-six years old—but making love with Hunter had been a giant step for her, one taken with commitment...on her side anyway. And now his sharp tone stung her to the quick, more so because she didn't understand it. It wasn't really surprising; she hadn't been a part of his world for long enough to play sophisticated games. She would just have to learn.

"I'm sorry. That was a hell of a crude thing to say!" But he didn't sound sorry. His words were clipped and abrupt.

"Yes." It came out as a whisper, but he heard.

"Gabby...."

"I'm sorry, Hunter, but I have to hang up now. Someone's at the door," she lied, desperate for an excuse. "Goodbye."

MIAMI WAS HOT and Charleston was rainy and hot. She hadn't been able to sleep even in the air-conditioned comfort of her rooms. She was tired—no, exhausted—and in a terrible temper.

When her plane landed at Washington National Airport, even Hunter's unexpectedly affectionate greeting did nothing to lighten the memory of a miserable seven days. On the contrary, his smile and tender kiss only aggravated her ill humor.

He hadn't bothered to call her all week, and after their last conversation she had tried to tell heself that she was glad. She didn't need his fluctuating moods.

Had she imagined herself in love with him? How foolish of her. He was very sensual, and the time in Atlanta had been exciting and wonderful, but if he thought they would simply pick up where they had left off, then he'd better rethink. She had done some soul searching during the past week. She'd recognized herself as a woman long overdue her sensuality. Hunter had quite adroitly played on that, but just because he was the first man to love her didn't mean he was the only man she'd ever love. She would learn to play the games so that he couldn't hurt her.

She wrote every day, often over a room-service dinner. Her writing had become important to her, more important than she could have imagined. A relationship of some sort would have to be continued with Hunter, but she was determined that it be purely professional.

She didn't realize she'd been staring until he cocked his head to one side and lifted a brow. "Gabriella?"

"Hello, Hunter." She greeted him quietly, silently fighting the sensations he evoked by simply being there. He was dressed casually, in deference to the heat, in a short-sleeved black polo shirt and lightweight khaki slacks.

He took her briefcase from unprotesting fingers and caught her hand in his. "Still mad at me, tiger?" he asked in that sexy voice that seemed to roll over her skin like warm oil. *Remember*, she told herself, *remember that he didn't call. Remember that he is the Great Hunter Graham and you are a writer to be pacified.*

She jerked her hand free and faced him. "Look, Hunter, let's get something straight—" Her voice rose on an irritable note.

He took her elbow and turned her again into the stream of people on the concourse. "Not here, Gabby," he ordered.

She looked around at the interested stares they were collecting and subsided.

Washington—indeed, the entire Eastern Seaboard—was suffering from a miserable heat wave. The taxi wasn't air conditioned and to Gabby that was the last straw. The heat was heavy on her shoulders, so she shrugged off the jacket of her white linen suit. Her irritation grew in direct proportion to the perspiration that wet her hair, stung her eyes and ran in rivulets between her breasts. Hunter looked as cool as the proverbial cucumber and she hated him for it. He must have slept like a log while she'd been tossing and turning.

Wisely he left her in peace. Had he spoken she was afraid she would embarrass them both by screaming at him.

When they reached the hotel he directed the doorman to send her bags up and led her past the desk toward the bank of elevators and into an empty car. The air conditioning was a blessed relief. At the eighth floor he indicated the direction she should take with a silent wave of his hand. This suite was larger and more elaborate than the one in Atlanta. The three bedrooms were clustered at the rear rather than being separated by the living room.

Hunter showed her to one of them and spoke directly to her for the first time since the airport. "Why don't you have a cool bath? Your bags should be up in a minute."

"Thank you." She glided past him into the room and closed the door in his face. Immediately she began to shed her clothes, leaving a trail across the floor to the bath.

The cool water was heavenly. A few hours of this and she might be almost human again, she thought as she sank beneath the water level and came up with her hair plastered to her head like a wet seal.

A knock on the door startled her and she sat up abruptly. The water churned, threatening to slosh over the sides of the long deep tub.

"Your bags are here, Gabby. I've ordered our lunch from room service, so if you don't feel like dressing...." He left the suggestive sentence hanging. Was he deliberately trying to provoke her further? The shiver that trembled through her sprang from the air conditioning and the cool bath, surely.

"I'll be out in a little while," she informed him shortly.

"WHEN ARE MOTHER AND DAPHNE ARRIVING?" Gabby asked an hour later. She'd dressed in a loose-fitting lightweight caftan of vivid turquoise. It was the most enveloping garment in her suitcase and the most comfortable. She left the table for a large easy chair, curling her feet under her. The lunch had been delicious—Crabmeat Louis followed by sweet raspberry sherbet. As she sipped a glass of iced tea she gave a sigh of repletion and almost smiled.

"They'll be here tonight at eight."

Before she could respond Hunter had plucked the glass from her hand and deposited it on the floor. "Now, Gabriella," he said as he planted stiff arms on either side of the chair, effectively penning her in. "I've said some things I've regretted, and apologized for them. I'm sincerely sorry. Are you ever going to forgive me?" The dark eyes appealed to her daringly, but with a fragment of hesitation, as though he were more insecure than he cared for her to know and hid it behind a false bravado.

The onslaught of his nearness was so sudden that Gabby had no time to establish a defense. She was helplessly caught in his gaze. She searched his expression, almost dizzy from his dangerous proximity, his intoxicating masculine scent. Though she longed to forgive him, to forget his indifferent treatment of her, the memory of the pain he'd inflicted was too fresh. There was no way she could blithely resume an intimate relationship with him without knowing where she stood.

When she finally spoke, it was in a halting murmur. "Hunter, I—"

"Answer me honestly, Gabriella," he demanded.

"Honestly?" She lifted a hand to his cheek. "I don't know whether I'm capable of honesty with you anymore, Hunter." Her eyes pleaded for his understanding. "You've taken me in over my depth." She finished in a whisper, "And left me there to drown."

With a half groan Hunter lifted her by the shoulders and took her place in the chair with her on his lap. Her long legs dangled over the corduroy arm.

It was the first time that a man had ever held her in his lap. After the initial shock she decided it was rather pleasant, if the man were as large as Hunter. A picture of herself planted on the lap of Steven Ward emerged and she had to stifle a grin. Steven was exactly her height and didn't weigh much more than she did. Sitting as she was now she would be looking down on the top of his head, whereas with Hunter she was able to meet his eyes.

"That's much better," Hunter told her huskily.

"What?"

"That smile. I wasn't sure I would ever see you

smile at me again, Gabby...and I hated the idea. I wouldn't leave you to drown. I've been through hell this week, sweetheart."

That surprised her. "You don't look like it."

Sunlight streamed in through a window at his back. As near as he was it threw his face into shadow, so she couldn't see his expression perfectly, but sincerity lowered his voice. "Gabby...."

"What, Hunter?"

WHAT, HE ASKED HIMSELF. What *could* he tell her? That he was probably falling in love for the first time in his life? That she was only beginning to blossom and deserved some freedom to enjoy herself, but that it tore his guts out to grant it? He wanted to wrap her in cotton wool, or sable, and keep her to himself.

"On the telephone, in Atlanta, you sounded very... casual...about what you called your 'research.'" He tried to relax his severe expression, remove the sternness from his voice. God, he sounded arrogant! Like the Great Hunter Graham she used to tease him about being.

Her gray eyes became wide enough to drown in. "And you took me seriously?" she breathed. "Those *boys*?" Her voice rose on the last word.

He finally managed a self-deprecating grin. "I'm afraid so. I was jealous, Gabby, and I took it very seriously." His hand slid across her back and up her nape into her hair.

The beautiful mouth curved into a sweet soft arc, and the lines of tension across her brow relaxed. "Oh, Hunter," she murmured, and buried her face in his neck.

His arms convulsed, bringing her closer. She felt

so damned good. He breathed in her scent, absorb-
ing it into his bloodstream. Her lips moved against
his throat, and he thought he would die if he didn't
have her. Now. But he schooled his desire with a
superhuman effort. She was speaking, not kissing
him.

"We've known each other for ten years, but we
don't know each other at all, do we?"

"Not like this," he agreed. Never like this.

She drew back and shook her head, but her lips
were smiling. She looked like a caricature of a
teacher, about to deliver a lecture to one of her students. And he felt that way—like a sixteen-year-old
boy with a beautiful woman in his arms.

"Gabby, listen to me. I deeply regret my suspicions...no, they weren't really suspicions; they
were fears."

Her brows arched inquiringly. "I can't imagine
your being afraid of anything."

He gave a husky laugh. "As you said, we don't
know each other very well." A deep breath, and he
went on, "Don't change, Gabby. You're unlike any
woman I've ever known, especially in your honesty.
My heart tells me that, but when you start to throw
out quips about what happened between us, my
heart closes down on me, and my mind warns that
you're as casual as any other woman. I didn't mean
to be cruel, sweetheart. I guess it was a form of self-
protection." And that was as much of an admission
of weakness in himself as he'd ever made before.

She was quiet for a minute. He let his head fall
back to rest wearily on the chair and closed his eyes.
"I didn't explain very well, did I?"

"You explained, but I don't think you made much

of an effort to understand me, Hunter," she told him softly.

The admonishment was enough to lift one lid. He peered at her warily.

"I waited twenty-six years," she finally went on. "Does that sound like I'm casual about sex? Do you think that just because you showed me something beautiful, I'll try to find it with everyone I meet? Or that it would be the same? That's unreasonable."

He lifted his head. His fingers at her nape tightened, bringing her lips to within a whisper of his. "Who the hell ever said love was reasonable?" he asked. There. It was out. For the first time in his life he had made himself vulnerable to someone else. For the first time he'd left himself wide open to the pain another person could cause. It scared the hell out of him.

"Love?" she whispered. The light in her eyes kindled to an incandescent flame, burning steadily. Maybe it was going to be all right.

"I love you, Gabby." He touched a finger to her lips. "My beautiful Gabriella." His mouth skimmed hers, his tongue teasing a corner of her lips. Why didn't she say something, he wondered. But then, when she opened her mouth, he blocked the words she might have uttered with his fingers. "I've missed you, tiger," he said roughly.

"Why didn't you call me?"

His lips began a trail down her cheek and across to tug gently at the lobe of her ear. "I wanted to give you plenty of time to forgive me. Besides, you hung up on me once," he growled against the skin of her neck. His tongue flicked out. God, she tasted good! One large hand cradled a breast "Who was at the door that night?" He drew away to look at her.

"AT THE DOOR? I don't...." Then Gabby remembered. "No one," she admitted, tilting her face up until it was only an inch from his.

His mouth hovered over her parted lips. "That was what I hoped," he ground out.

Suddenly he was kissing her with all the pent-up desire she felt. The heat from his body swirled around and into her, warming her from inside and out. Her hands slid into his hair as he stood with her in his arms. She was only vaguely aware that he'd moved. Her ears were filled with the thrilling sound of his whispered words of desire; her body, with the glorious heat of their mutual need, their love.

The mattress gave under his weight as he came down on one knee to place her gently on the bed. He propped himself on stiff arms over her. "I'm going to say this one more time, Gabriella Constant. I love you. You need breathing space to get used to the idea of being desirable, and I'm not going to push you, but I want you to know that I've never said those words to another woman. You're beautiful and I love you." He bent his elbows, lowering himself until he was a whisper away from her lips.

Gabby lost herself in his ardent gaze. "That's Lily. She's beautiful to you because you created her," she said with one last protest.

He grinned crookedly. "You see what I mean? No, darling, it's Gabby, too. She's beautiful inside, as well, and I love them both. We'll get to know each other in every way there is, as lovers, as friends; and I'll convince you."

"I believe I'm convinced," Gabby murmured huskily, and reached for him. Her body cried out for fulfillment of longings so recently discovered. Her pulse began to throb, anticipating his lovemaking with an impatience that lent speed to her hands tugging at the tails of his shirt.

He pulled the front zipper of the caftan down with fingers that were trembling noticeably. At the sight of her unencumbered breasts his eyes darkened to black pools of yearning. "Oh, sweetheart, I've wanted you, missed you so," he breathed. He slid the soft fabric from her shoulders, but before he could remove it completely the temptation before him became too much to resist. He abandoned the task to catch her breasts in his hands, burrowing his face into the scented valley between.

"You smell so delectable, like sunshine...and violets." He mouthed his way to a rosy-tipped nipple and tugged slightly with his lips. "I want you so much." His hot breath on her skin liquefied the bone and sinew of her body, leaving her pliable in his hands.

Her fingers tangled in the dark silken hair and held his head possessively. She gave a husky seductive laugh. "You're always trying to make love to me with your clothes on. Don't you think it would be easier without them?"

He lifted his head. She watched as his mouth curved into a blurred smile. His eyes were slightly dazed, but he managed a faint laugh. "Sorry. I got sidetracked," he said.

She lifted her hips to accommodate him as he pulled the caftan free. It sailed across the room to be followed by her sheer bikini panties. His eyes feasted upon her while he pulled the shirt over his head and stepped out of the rest of his clothes in one hurried movement.

A breathless tension gripped her at the sight of his magnificent body, eagerly aroused. She lifted her arms and he came down to cover her, thigh to thigh, breast to breast, his mouth seeking hers, his arms underneath her, molding her soft shape to the hard planes of his hips. Her body complied as though it had memorized the fit.

"This is where you should have been instead of on that damned tour. Here in my arms." He began a slow tortuous journey down her body with his hands, his lips, blazing a trail of molten desire, demanding an answering passion. She gave it willingly.

When his fingers reached her thighs they curved inward to the throbbing core of her desire, moist, warm, welcoming. She cried out and reached for him. "Now, Hunter...oh, please, now."

He eased between her legs, letting her accept him at her own pace, his breathing shallow and uneven. His lids had drifted shut, and she could see the soft throb of the pulse in his neck even as she felt it under her palms where they moved restlessly on his chest. His heartbeat was strong and vibrant. "Gabby, oh, Gabby, love..." he whispered.

She reached around his neck to pull his face down to her parted lips at the same moment that her back arched, and she received all the glory of his manhood.

His hips began a slow, purposeful undulation that gradually increased to an erotic rhythm of desire and growing sensation. Stretching, reaching to seize the full range of passion, they strained, breath caught, until they spanned the scope of all feeling in one exhilarating, extended moment of climax.

They touched down gently, stroking each other with loving caresses, whispering phrases meaningless except to two lovers on their return to reality from that most remarkable of all journeys.

Hunter propped himself over her on his elbows and smoothed a damp tendril from her forehead. "I love you," he murmured, covering her lips with a kiss of infinite tenderness.

Gabby smiled. Her hands moved up and down his back with a gentle restless touch. She started to echo his words, but something, some lingering remnant of disquiet, held her back.

Finally he rolled onto his side as though reluctant to leave the embrace of her warm thighs. Holding her under one arm with her head resting on his chest, he combed his fingers through her hair.

She ran a flat palm across the wiry hair on his chest before tucking her hand under her cheek and letting her eyes drift shut.

THERE WAS ANOTHER SUBJECT that had been on her mind all week. After they had showered, and Hunter was dressing to go to the convention hall for a preliminary check, she broached it. She took a breath and let it out, blurting, "What about Gabby's manuscript? Have you read it?"

In the mirror she saw his hands falter as he was knotting a dark blue tie under the collar of a lighter blue shirt. "I've been busy," he evaded. "Getting ready for the ABA convention always puts me weeks behind. Are you sure you won't go with me?"

Raising herself on one elbow, she smiled into the mirror. "Like this?" She hadn't dressed yet. The folds of the cranberry lace negligee she wore left one long leg bare. She lifted her leg slightly and wiggled her toes at him.

He grinned. "You do plan to dress before I take you out for dinner, I hope."

"Maybe." She rolled onto her back. "I don't believe you answered my question," she said tentatively, not looking at him.

"Sweetheart, I'm in a hurry to get this business done and get back here to you. Could we talk about it later?" he asked briskly.

She began to have the most awful premonition, but she persisted anyway. "Hunter, I started the research for that book in college. It's taken me over a year to write it. Surely you must have glanced through it." He finally turned to face her, and her expression chided him for an answer.

Hunter gave a resigned sigh. "Honestly?" he asked.

She nodded.

"The book is really bad, Gabby. I can't publish it," he said finally.

Gabby didn't answer. She simply lay gazing up at him, stunned.

Hunter came to sit on the bed beside her. "Sweetheart, you do romance really well." He couldn't resist a smile at the double meaning. "Your love scenes are moving and sensual; your characters are totally believable. Why don't you stick to a genre that pays you well and in which you excel? You entertained a lot of people with *Captive*."

"You don't think I could do rewrites?" she offered.

He put an arm across her waist. "There's no point in lying to you, Gabby. Absolutely not. The manuscript was lousy."

She bristled at his tone and started to roll away, but his arm tightened.

"If I've made you mad, I'm sorry. But I don't want to raise false hopes and see you hurt."

Her hair fell over her shoulder as she swung her head to face him. "You don't think you've hurt me by saying that my book is lousy?" she accused.

Hunter became very still. "And you hurt me when you don't trust my judgment. Don't you think I would publish your book if I could justify it? Write me another romance and I'll have it out so fast it will make your head spin," he said bluntly. "You don't have to mold opinion, Gabby, or make a statement to society. Simply entertain people. It's what we need more of today. Romance is a viable form of literature. Look at the millions of women who read it regularly."

"And look at the millions of dollars it makes for you!" she spat, her anger growing. She knew she should stop, think what she was saying, but somehow she couldn't. The words poured out and once out couldn't be recalled. "You know what I think, Hunter? I think you just want the money I'll bring in with another romance!"

The muscle in his jaw gave a jump, then became rigid. "Of course I do. Publishing is my business. If I don't make money, I'm out of work." He tried to joke, but it was a miserable effort.

Gabby faltered. Her book! The book that she'd worked so hard on.... She wanted to hurl herself into his arms and cry, but she couldn't. An awful thought surfaced. Had he told her he loved her to soften the blow? She slid off the bed and crossed quickly to the bathroom door. "I'm sure Nina will find someone who likes it."

Hunter didn't answer.

10

WHEN GABBY REENTERED THE BEDROOM, Hunter had left for the convention hall. She slipped into the more concealing caftan before going to the telephone.

"Nina Worth, please," she said to the switchboard operator at the agency in New York. "This is Gabby Constant."

"Hello, Gabby," Nina greeted her. "Are you in Washington?"

"Yes, I got here this morning. Nina I—"

"I'm sure Hunter was there waiting," Nina said. "He was *very* impatient to see—"

Gabby could almost see her suggestive grin. "Nina, I want to ask you something," she broke in.

"Certainly."

Was that reserve in her agent's voice? Gabby sank onto the side of the bed. Her fingers played over the rumpled sheets. "Hunter said he'd send you a copy of my new manuscript. Did he?"

"Uh, yes, he did."

"And...and what did you...?" She swallowed. "How did you like it?"

Suddenly Nina was all business. "Don't ask," she said dryly. "It would never sell, Gabby. Why don't you stick to what you do well?"

Almost the same words that Hunter had used! A

suspicion began to take root in her mind. "Did you and Hunter talk, Nina?"

"Yes, we did. I'm your agent, so naturally he called me. Hunter won't publish that one, Gabby."

"I know. He's already told me." Gabby felt weary and miserable. "Will you try to sell it to someone else?"

"I'm sorry, honey, but nobody is going to want that book. I agree with Hunter."

"Of course you do. Neither of you would make much money on a history of turn-of-the-century America," Gabby snapped.

"Oh, Gabby! It's not that." Nina sounded tired, too.

"Isn't it?" Gabby said stiffly, not giving an inch.

"Listen to me. Stop trying to live in your mother's shadow. You are not Henrietta," Nina lectured sternly. "Don't try to write like her!"

Gabby was shocked at that. She had never tried to be like Henrietta. Never! Nina was just making excuses to hide the real reason for her dislike of the history book: the money she stood to make if Gabriella Constant remained Lily Andore. Well, Gabby refused to do that.

"I'm writing history, the way I should have done before. If you can't represent me on the new book, then I don't need you to represent me in anything."

There was a long silence on the other end. "I'm sorry you feel that way, Gabby."

"I'm sorry, too, Nina. Goodbye."

When she hung up she curled into a ball of misery on the bed and let the tears flow until finally she fell asleep.

GABBY HEARD HER UNEXPECTED CHAMPION before she saw her. "Why is she sleeping at this time of the evening?"

Rolling over, she looked at the slit of light under the door. "Mother?" she murmured. A deep rolling sound was indecipherable except as a male voice.

"Have you upset her, Hunter?" Henrietta asked, obviously into the role of suspicious parent.

Gabby came off the bed like a shot. Her mother mustn't.... She reached the door at the same moment that it swung inward. Enfolded in loving arms, she had to bend to kiss her mother's cheek, but for the first time in what seemed like years she felt like a little girl again.

"My dear," her mother said warmly. "I'm so very glad to see you." She flipped the light switch on the wall and closed the door in Hunter's face.

Gabby had a momentary glimpse of his grim features, and Daphne standing behind him looking confused.

"You must be exhausted, Gabby," Henrietta continued as she peeled off her gloves. "My goodness! You did have a nap, didn't you?"

Horrified, Gabby followed her mother's gaze to the rumpled sheets, the spread trailing on the floor, the pillows. *Oh, my God!* "Well, I, er...."

"Never mind." Henrietta waved a dismissive hand and changed the subject.

Gabby was suddenly overwhelmed with her love for this dainty but iron-hard, loyal little lady. "Mother, I love you," she said. One large tear escaped to trail through the streaks of others down her face.

"I love you, too, dear, but you mustn't cry," Henrietta instructed. She settled into a chair of slipper satin, arranged her skirts like some regal belle and fixed Gabby with a speculative regard. "I want to hear all about it."

Gabby hesitated for only a moment—surely Henrietta was not playing a part now—and then she told her *almost* everything. She feared her mother would read between the lines, but if Henrietta suspected that her daughter had earlier been tumbled on the very bed where she now sat cross-legged, she never let on.

In the middle of the recital, Hunter knocked on the door. "Gabby?" he called.

Henrietta indicated that Gabby should keep her seat. She swung open the door and faced him with one fist planted firmly on her hip. "Yes?" she said coolly.

Hunter's eyes sought Gabby where she sat. His expression was unreadable, but he couldn't seem to look away from her. She tried to hold her composure in the force of that gaze, but finally her shoulders slumped under its weight.

Only then did he speak. "We have dinner reservations downstairs in half an hour. Are you going to join us?" he asked.

Henrietta turned to her daughter. "Gabby?"

Gabby could hear voices from the living room of the suite. Hunter answered her question before she could ask it. "Chastain Conway and Diana James are here." The mystery writer and the restaurant critic—they both had books to be released by Graham House in the near future and they were to appear at the convention.

She made an instant decision. "You go, mother. I think I'll just have something sent up."

Henrietta straightened to her full height. "I'll stay with Gabby. We still have a lot of catching up to do," she said to the stone-faced man before her, and then added sweetly, "Besides, I haven't yet read her new manuscript."

Storm clouds gathered on Hunter's brow. He gave both of them a mocking bow and left.

HOURS LATER Gabby lay staring at the ceiling. The long nap that afternoon had left her wide awake. A warm soak in the tub hadn't helped, and she knew that her insomnia was as much the result of the arguments with Hunter and Nina as of the nap.

Henrietta had pronounced the manuscript "marvelous" after reading only one chapter. Her opinion had made Gabby feel better at first, until she'd realized that Henrietta would think anything her daughter wrote was "marvelous." That reflection had only added to her depression.

Maybe a glass of wine would make her sleepy. She had noticed a well-stocked refrigerator in the tiny bar. She got up and pulled on the cranberry lace peignoir over its matching nightgown.

The living room of the suite was dimly lit and deserted. Gabby browsed through the refrigerator and came up with a Riesling. After struggling manfully with the cork, she poured the wine into a stemmed glass and wandered around the room, bottle in one hand, glass in the other. The light fruity taste was pleasant to her palate. She took another sip and sat down at the game table in front of the window.

The lighted Washington Monument pointed at a full moon over the tops of the cherry trees that lined the mall below. American history of any period was a viable ɹrm of literature, too, she told the empty room, even if the Great Hunter Graham didn't agree.

A deck of cards, provided by the hotel, caught her eye. She set the bottle beside her glass on the table before her and picked up the pack to strip off the cellophane.

The cards were stiff and new in her hands as she shuffled them. Almost absently she began to deal them out.

Solitaire. How appropriate, she thought sorrowfully, and took another sip of wine. The red ten on the black jack on the red queen—and the whole thing on the black king. Hunter Graham was the black king.

Suddenly a key rattled in the lock of the door that led to the hallway, and there he stood. The jacket of his black tuxedo was caught in two fingers over his shoulder. The ends of his bow tie dangled from under his opened collar.

He hesitated when he saw her, but then turned to close the door almost silently. He tossed the jacket on a nearby chair and the key landed on top of it. His hands slid into the pockets of his trousers, and he sauntered toward the table where she sat. "Couldn't sleep?" he asked casually.

Gabby had to swallow before she could answer. "No. I thought a glass of wine might relax me." Nervously she looped her hair behind her ear. If only he weren't so damned sexy, and virile, and seductive. She made herself remember her book.

One large hand came out of his pocket to wrap around the neck of the bottle. He lifted it to examine the label. "Good year," he proclaimed. "May I?"

She nodded. "Of course. You're paying for it."

He went to the bar for a glass and poured the wine before taking the chair opposite hers. "Want to play some gin?"

Gabby had to smile. Two antagonists sat across the table from each other at three o'clock in the morning, sipping wine and playing cards. It might have been a Humphrey Bogart movie. "That depends on the stakes," she told him mildly.

Hunter lazed in the chair, hooking one arm over the back. His dark hooded gaze held hers. "Oh, lady," he breathed almost inaudibly. "You left yourself wide open with that one. But I'll let you get away with it this once."

To hide the sudden shaking of her hands, Gabby gathered up the cards and began to shuffle them again. When they were well mixed she squared the corners of the deck and placed it on the table in front of him. She watched, fascinated, as he stretched out a hand to cut the cards. Her wayward mind could only see those hands as they roamed her body, and the memory sent shivers through her. This wasn't a good idea, but with a brisk motion she began to deal. She turned one card, the three of diamonds, up beside the pack.

Hunter picked up his cards and fanned them out. One dark brow quirked in amusement as he studied them. "What is it they say? 'Lucky at cards...'?" He picked up the three and laid down his hand. "Gin."

Gabby threw her own cards down in disgust. "Unlucky in love." The rest of the quotation beat through her blood with the rhythm of hope. Ridiculous, she scolded herself.

Hunter linked his fingers together and leaned for-

ward on his forearms. "What did Henrietta think of
your manuscript?"

Gabby tilted her chin. "She loved it."

"I'm sure she did." He took one of her hands between his broad palms, warming her fingers with a
slight back-and-forth motion.

Was he going to apologize? Gabby felt her heart
reach out expectantly. "Gabby, let me say something. We're here for the booksellers' convention.
They are important to all of us in this business. The
man who has one store in a town of three thousand
is just as important as the huge nationwide chains.
They come every year to see what we, the publishers, have to offer them, and I won't cheat them
by offering less than the best.

"You know, tiger, I never figured you for one who
would run to mother."

"I'm not!" She snatched her hand away.

"No?" he questioned. "Did I miss something? The
two of you were shut up in your bedroom for hours."

"I . . . it's just . . . she would never betray me," she
blurted. Less than the best?

"Betray you? Is that what I've done? Because I re-
fuse to publish a bad book?"

Gabby got to her feet. "That's only your opinion,"
she snapped in a voice that made it clear how important she thought his opinion was.

"Gabby, trust me," he urged quietly. "I only want
what's best for you."

His constraint only served to fuel her anger. "Or
what's best for Graham House?" she sneered, furious now beyond reason. Her hands were flat on the
table and she glared down at him. "Mother says that
I can find another publisher very easily."

She watched the muscle in his jaw clench. He was silent for a minute, then he asked with suspicious calm, "Oh? And whom does she recommend?"

"She suggested that I talk to Peter Gordon."

Hunter inhaled sharply. She knew that she had scored a hit. Peter Gordon was his biggest rival. His eyes narrowed to dangerous slits. When he spoke his voice was dangerous, too, but smooth and silky.

"I'm sure that Peter Gordon will have a proposition for you." His eyes dropped suggestively to her breasts. "I wonder how far you'll be willing to go to see the book in print."

Gabby's face flooded with violent color as she straightened. "It appears you don't trust me very much, either. Thanks for the warning. Am I to assume that all publishers are sneaking, conniving lechers?"

It was as though a mask had descended over his face—a hard, expressionless mask. "Well, now I know how you really feel about me," he said woodenly.

"Oh, were you in doubt?" she asked airily, though her knees were shaking. "You should have asked."

One hand raked impatiently through his hair. "Are you this mad just because I won't publish the damned book?"

"Yes! That book is good!" she lashed out. "I know it's good! It may not make much money, but it covers facts from a period of history that hasn't been thoroughly explored. It does have value."

Hunter stood, towering over her in her bare feet. "Why the hell do you think that period hasn't been thoroughly explored? Because it's dull, boring—just like your damned book! And if you hadn't turned

into such a prima donna you'd have the objectivity
to see that!" he roared.

"A prima donna? Why you...you...arrogant—"
she sputtered.

A door opened at the end of the hall. Daphne's
head poked out. "For heaven's sake, you two! Do
you want to wake up Henrietta?" she hissed.

"My mother sleeps like the dead. A ground-zero
blast wouldn't wake her. But you're right, Daphne—this conversation is fruitless. Good night!"

It was a superb exit line, but before she could leave
he had her wrist in an iron-hard grip. "Listen." He
rubbed his eyes with a tired gesture. "Okay. I'll publish the book. A small print run."

Gabby knew a horrible pain in her heart, which
she could feel molding her features to a hard mask.
"Don't patronize me, Hunter," she said through lips
that were stiff with the effort not to cry. "That's the
worst insult of all."

"Dammit! I'm not!"

"Have you changed your mind about the value
of...of...." She waved a hand.

His hand moved around to massage the back of
his neck. He looked down at her with the saddest
expression she'd ever seen.

She wanted to comfort him, to draw him into her
arms, to fold him into a tight embrace and stroke
him until his pain, and hers, was eased. But she
couldn't.

Finally he shook his head. "No," he whispered.

"Good night, Hunter."

PETER GORDON was quite handsome and charming, so
why did she feel almost repulsed by him? Because of

Hunter's innuendo, she supposed. She made a conscious effort to warm her smile across the dinner table the next night.

Hunter had been busy all day with promotional details now that the conference had officially opened. Gabby had been relieved of his presence, and it was a comforting deliverance.

"When can I see the manuscript, Gabby?" Peter asked.

"I have a copy in the suite. I can get it for you after dinner, Mr. Gordon."

"Peter, please." He reached for her hand.

She had to steel herself not to jerk away and hide it in her lap. "Peter."

"I have a feeling that I'm going to love it," he said in an ingratiating tone.

Gabby squirmed uncomfortably. "I hope so. I feel that it has merit. Unfortunately my former publisher didn't agree. That's why I'm looking for a new one."

"And you came to the right person. I'm quite a history buff myself. I can hardly wait to read it. Will you be submitting it under your real name?"

"Oh, yes! I think Lily Andore is much too frivolous for a history book. Besides, it conjures up a certain, ah...."

"Notoriety?" Peter finished for her. His thumb was lightly tracing her knuckles. "I understand," he said sympathetically. "I did think Hunter was using you rather badly when he sent you off across the country like that."

"Did I hear my name?" A hearty voice spoke from behind them. "No, no! Don't get up, Peter."

"I wasn't going to," Peter told him shortly.

"So the renowned Lily Andore is moving on to

greener pastures," Hunter said as if he didn't find the thought annoying at all. Gabby couldn't help noticing, though, that he glared at their clasped hands.

She focused all her attention on Peter, rewarding him with her sweetest smile. "If Peter likes the manuscript," she said.

"Oh, he'll like it," Hunter grated in a low voice.

"I'm sure I will," agreed Peter smoothly. "I'm looking forward to a very...close...relationship with Lily—uh, Gabby."

"Well, that's one distinction you'd better get straight. Miss Constant doesn't like it when you confuse the two."

Peter smiled an apology, but Gabby felt his tension through the fingers that still held hers. "I'll get it straight."

Hunter clapped him on the back. "You won't be disappointed, but let me warn you, buddy." His dark eyes took on a burning glow, pinning Gabby in her chair, and his voice dropped a whole octave. "She takes notes."

A gasp of pure fury slipped out.

But Hunter had moved on to greet someone at the next table. Short of making a scene, she couldn't very well give him the benefit of her observations about his character.

Peter looked bewildered. "What did he mean by that?"

"Nothing!" Gabby snapped. "Nothing at all, Peter. Let's go." She rose and stalked out.

By the time Peter had paid the check and caught up with her, some of her ire had cooled, but she was still in no mood to be charming.

Peter Gordon walked with her to the suite, was given the manuscript and shown the door.

How could he? How could he do such a thing, she seethed as she paced. She waited up long past the time when her mother and Daphne came in, but Hunter didn't appear. Finally she went to bed.

11

THE HUGE HALL was packed with convention-goers, there for business and fun. And the publishers were supplying both. Some of the booths were beautiful fantasies, others used the high-tech sales approach.

Gabby threaded her way through the throng to the booth of Gordon Publishing Company.

Peter was deep in conversation with a blond woman in a red dress. When she turned Gabby recognized her immediately as an author of contemporary romance fiction, but couldn't put a name with the face.

Peter saw Gabby and hurried forward to greet her. The woman followed at a slower pace. The reason for her reluctance was immediately apparent: they had on the same dress, the red silk that Gabby loved and wore so often. She gave the woman an apologetic smile and was told with a grin that she had excellent taste.

The remark served to remind her that the credit was really due to Hunter, not herself. Memories surfaced, of Jacques and Marie and that intense week of makeover that had left her feeling a bit like a sybarite. March in New York seemed to belong to another lifetime, a softer, more innocent time, when her world had centered on one hundred forty-two boisterous sixteen-year-olds.

They would be out for summer vacation now. Did any of them ever think of her? *For heaven's sake, Gabby, don't go maudlin.* She recalled her straying thoughts in response to Peter's, "Gabby?"

"Yes, Peter?"

"I said I loved the book."

"You've read it?" That was certainly flattering. If he was half as busy as Hunter, when had he found the time?

"Of course! It was wonderful."

"The whole thing?"

"Every word. I'm so proud to have the honor of publishing it, Gabby. It will make quite a splash in the academic world."

The comment warmed her all the way through and, she had to admit, fostered a feeling of great relief. In the back of her mind had been that nagging question: were Hunter and Nina right? Even when she refused to accept their verdict she had wondered at disregarding the opinions of two people she thought she could trust. Her spirits soared. "Oh, thank you, Peter. You don't know what this means to me."

"And to me," he enthused—a little too happily?—and rubbed his hands together in the manner of a person who expects a large amount of money to come his way.

Gabby shrugged. She tried not to let her doubt interfere with her gratitude as she thanked him again. He had confirmed her own judgment, after all. She chastised herself for always looking for problems where none existed.

"I want to get things settled immediately, Gabby, so I've already called our contracts department.

They'll draw up the papers today and send them down by courier. They should be here tomorrow."

Tomorrow? Why was he in such a hurry? "Fine, Peter," she agreed, but soon after she wandered off, wanting to be alone with her thoughts.

As she walked slowly down an aisle, someone thrust a book into her hands.

So Peter had already read her manuscript, had he? When?

A well-dressed woman offered her a green canvas tote bag with the familiar logo of a line of children's books. She took it, smiling her thanks vaguely.

He had left her at the suite at ten. Maybe he was a speed reader. A bronzed Indian complete with beads and loincloth appeared from out of nowhere to place a feather band around her head and another book in her hand. She looked straight through him and dropped both books into the bag.

He would *have* to be a speed reader to have got through seven hundred plus pages. She thought back over the conversation. A splash in the academic world? She doubted that. It was a nice history, packed with little-known facts of the period, but it was not a definitive work. She'd never intended it to be.

A huge person blocked her way, forcing her to look up. "Isn't that getting a little heavy?" Hunter asked.

She looked down at the bag. It was filled with books, pens, posters, bookmarks, calendars. Where had all that stuff come from? While she stood in confusion a man in a chef's costume came up to them and handed her a flyer proclaiming the glories of a new cookbook—and a chocolate chip cookie. Absently she took a bite.

"They think you're a bookseller," Hunter went on to inform her coolly. "I hope you're going to take off your headdress before your autographing."

She looked up at him with a vacant stare. She still hadn't spoken, but her mind was racing. Peter hadn't read that book.

"Gabby? Are you all right?" Hunter's scowl was suddenly touched with concern. His fingers curled around her arm. "Gabby? Sweetheart, are you all right?"

She jerked her arm free. "Take this!" She pushed the bag at him and pivoted on her heel back in the direction from where she'd come.

"Gabby, you're autographing is in ten minutes!" Hunter called after her furiously.

"I'll be there," she threw back over her shoulder with an abstracted carelessness.

DAMN HER! She was still a sassy brat. He watched her long legs take her away from him and the sight suddenly seemed symbolic. Well, good riddance, he thought, jamming his hands into his pockets. Gabby Constant could certainly take care of herself. He didn't have to worry about her. And wouldn't, he vowed. He knew Peter Gordon.

But she had looked so pale for a minute; had she...? He couldn't complete the thought. Last night he'd been unable to face a return to the suite, maybe to find her gone. He'd walked the streets of Washington until dawn, hoping that if he went far enough his heart might begin to beat again, he might be able to take a breath without feeling as if a knife had penetrated his chest.

Why the *hell* had he let himself fall in love? After

all these years, after all the marriages he'd watched end in disaster, including his own parents', he should have known better.

His face took on the hardness of resolve. He'd always known women were trouble when you let them get too close. He'd definitely let Gabby get too close, but never again. He didn't need that. He didn't need her. He didn't need *anyone* permanently.

He made his thoughts deliberately crude, harsh. Good-looking broads were a dime a dozen. There were plenty of women out there waiting, women who could be bought with a bauble. Gabby's price was too high. She wanted his professional integrity, and he wouldn't pay that. She wasn't willing to trust his judgment, to trust *him*.

He was lucky he'd found out before there was a ring on her finger, before she'd had his child. The sudden picture of Gabby with a child in her arms brought a fresh wave of pain.

No! Dammit, no! He swung around sharply and headed for the booth to take care of some business for a change. Love was for other men, not for him. He'd got along very well without it for years, and he'd get along without it from now on.

PETER WAS IN THE SAME SPOT and so was the woman in the red dress. Marietta de Free, that was her name, thought Gabby uselessly. "Peter, may I have a word with you." She grabbed his arm and practically manhandled him along toward the back of the booth. "Will you excuse me, Miss de Free?" she called back over her shoulder.

"Certainly," said the woman with a rather puzzled smile.

"Peter," Gabby began sweetly, "would you give me just a hint of what will be in my contract."

He smiled broadly. "Money. I wondered why you hadn't asked about your advance." He named a figure that was staggering and looked very pleased with himself.

Gabby's mouth fell open. "My book couldn't possibly earn back that advance!"

"Of course not, but with joint accounting on your next two...uh, you probably don't understand all this business talk," he said indulgently. She was surprised that he didn't pat her on the head.

"Joint accounting!" she squeaked. "What two books?"

"Why, your next two Lily Andore books. I'm offering a three-book contract. We'll more than make up our losses."

Gabby straightened to her full height and took a deep breath. She looked him squarely in the eye. "I know what joint accounting means, Peter; I am not an imbecile! The profits from future works make up any losses you might incur on one book."

It was Peter's turn to be surprised, but he recovered quickly. "You believe in this manuscript, don't you, Gabby?"

She hesitated.

"If we should suffer a slight loss, wouldn't you be willing to let the works of Lily Andore pay for this fine venture?"

Her smoky gray eyes hardened to pewter. "Peter, what period of history did I write about?"

"Well, I uh—"

"Did you even read the book, Peter?" she de-

manded. Her spirits were toppling, plunging to meet
the depths of her humiliation. "Did you?"

"Gabby, this is business." He was grasping now,
and the sight turned her stomach. "You should leave
it all to your agent."

Tears blurred his figure. "Thanks to my own stu-
pidity I no longer have an agent. So I'll just have to
make the decision myself. I will not sign your contract, Peter." She pronounced each word deliberately.

"Now, Gabby—"

"Did you read any of it?" She tried to sound
strong, but to add to her discredit the words came
out querulous and fussy.

There was silence for a moment and then Peter
gave a resigned sigh. "Nine or ten pages," he admitted with a dry smile. "They were the most boring
pages I've ever read."

A WHITE-FACED GABBY took her place at the table ten
minutes later. Hunter had provided books for her to
autograph and give away to the booksellers. She
looked up into the first face and gave a bright smile.
"What is your name?" she asked the man.

"Floyd Robertson, Miss Andore," he answered eagerly. "Robertson's Books in Portland, Maine. I hope
you'll make Portland a stop on your next tour."

"To Floyd with all good wishes," she wrote, and
signed with a flourish, "Lily Andore."

"I certainly will, Mr. Robertson. Thank you for
wanting me."

Finally the hour was over. Gabby headed directly
to the booth that sported a large red banner—Graham House, Inc.

Hunter sat at a table talking to two men with badges that proclaimed them representatives of one of the largest bookselling chains in America.

Gabby stood on one foot and then the other, impatient to get this over with. The lock of hair fell over his forehead, and she longed to push it away. She watched his lips move as he spoke and ached to feel them on hers. He had to forgive her. He had to! She had been so criminally stupid—but surely he would understand.

The men got up to leave. A woman was waiting, but before she could take a chair, a desperate Gabby excused herself and asked for just one minute of Hunter's time.

"This is the business of the convention, Gabby. I hope you have a good reason to interrupt," he grated. The muscle in his jaw jumped as he glared down at her. "I don't like to keep these people waiting."

"I need to talk to you," she pleaded.

With an apologetic smile at the woman, Hunter dragged her behind a screen.

"Did Gordon accept your manuscript?" he asked in a voice like frozen steel.

Her face flooded with rosy color. "Yes, but—"

At the sight of the blush, his hard hands came out to grasp her shoulders. He gave her a shake. "I could wring your neck! So you did whatever was necessary? I almost feel sorry for the poor fellow. I know what it feels like to be used!" he snarled.

"Used?" she said blankly. "I don't understand."

"You very graciously let me make love to you in Atlanta and then handed me your manuscript. Did you do the same for Peter?"

Her mouth opened, then closed again. Her eyes were wide with wretchedness. "Would it do me any good to deny it?" she asked.

"No! I don't give a damn what you had to do to get that contract! As far as I'm concerned, Lily Andore is more trouble than she's worth. I don't care whether I ever see her again."

His voice and blistering gaze were scathingly intent, slashing into her, leaving her numb with pain. "And Gabby Constant?" she ventured.

For a moment his eyes seemed to go wild with an emotion she'd never seen before. His large hands tightened on her upper arms, hurting, but the discomfort was nothing compared to what she felt in her heart.

"Gabby is a spoiled, selfish brat who can't see beyond her own ego! And now, if you'll excuse me, I'll get back to the important people I told you about."

Her throat burned with unshed tears. She longed for the relief of letting them fall, but from somewhere deep inside came the strength not to. He really did think that she would stoop to the methods he was accusing her of. She should be furious, but oddly she wasn't. What she felt was the most terrible, heartrending torment and regret.

Hunter had offered her love. In her own self-assertion she had repaid him by denying him her trust and never confessing her own love. From the expression on his face she correctly surmised that it was too late for that now, and he would never offer himself again. "I think I'll go back to New York this afternoon. My part in this is all over."

A chaos of emotions chased across his face, but his

voice was as colorless as hers when he spoke. "As you wish."

The next huge hurdle was to get out of there with some degree of aplomb. She started to turn away, but to her dismay he didn't release her. He pulled her slowly, reluctantly against him and covered her gasp of surprise with his mouth. The kiss was not tender, or loving, but a well-executed benediction for all they had meant to each other, and she responded with the same sad hunger.

When he lifted his head he seemed more angry with himself than with her. "Stay away from trouble," he warned harshly. "I won't be around anymore to pull you out of the scrapes your mouth gets you into." Unbidden, his eyes went to that mouth before he gave a snort of disgust and thrust her away as though he couldn't bear to touch her.

12

THE TRIP HOME was a painful haze, and when Gabby finally fit the key into her front door she was overwhelmingly grateful for the empty house upstairs. Mrs. James was taking her vacation, and her mother would have to remain in Washington until after her own autograph session, scheduled for Thursday. Gabby had two days to pull herself together—if it was possible. She'd thought she was so damned smart! She had managed to throw away the most important thing in her life over useless pride. An inflated opinion of her own judgment had cost her Hunter's love.

She went for long walks in Central Park, letting the unrelenting June heat wave, now in its second week, sap her energy in hopes that she would sleep. But when sleep came it was no comfort. Her dreams were all of Hunter. She would wake in the wee hours of the morning to pace through the empty rooms of her apartment, searching for something, anything, to take her thoughts away from him. The first night found her in the kitchen at 2:00 A.M., following an unbelievably complicated .recipe for a chocolate bombe.

She picked up books and discarded them, turned the television on and off and on again. It wasn't easy, but gradually she gained a modicum of control.

She called Nina and was forgiven much too easily.

"Will you take me back as a client if I promise not to submit that horrible book?" she sniffed.

"Of course I will, Gabby," Nina said warmly. "As a matter of fact, why don't you try a novel set in that period? It's a shame to let the research go to waste."

"Maybe," Gabby wavered. "But you'll have to find me another publisher. I'm afraid Hunter has washed his hands...." Her voice faltered and trailed off. She bit down hard on her lip, shut her eyes tight and gripped the telephone with straining fingers. If simply saying his name out loud produced this effect, how was she going to get through the rest of her life?

Nina chuckled. "I'm not so sure of that. He called me this morning."

Gabby's eyes flew open. "He did?"

"Yes. He warned me that you might be getting in touch. Hunter heard that you didn't sign Peter's contract."

So that was why Nina hadn't seemed surprised by her call.

"H-how did he sound?" Gabby had to ask.

"Like a bear ready to chew nails," Nina said cheerfully. "He threatened to cut off all business with our agency if I submitted anything on your behalf."

"Oh." Well, she wasn't surprised. That was more or less what he'd said to her, too.

"It was rather a strange call," Nina mused aloud. "He seemed disappointed that I hadn't already heard from you."

"I had to build up my courage," Gabby told her. "It isn't very palatable—humble pie."

Nina laughed.

Henrietta called twice during the two days. Gabby had left her a short note when she flew home from Washington. Henrietta didn't mention Hunter, but from her conversation Gabby gathered that there was a tension in the suite in Washington that her mother did nothing to ease.

Late Thursday afternoon Henrietta returned in a flutter of maternal concern.

Gabby heard the taxi and the slam of the front door above her. Sure enough, in five minutes Henrietta was downstairs. Wearing a wide determined smile and a flowered apron, Gabby greeted her at the door. "I'm glad you're home, mother. Come in."

"Gabby, dear." Her mother kissed her and eyed the apron. "Where's Mrs. James?" she asked. "The house seems empty."

"She won't be back until tomorrow. I'm your cook tonight. Chicken Suprême à Blanc and chocolate mousse!"

"Sounds delicious," said Henrietta. She studied her daughter very closely, but evidently found nothing amiss — or nothing she cared to comment on at the moment. Gabby was grateful. Arm in arm they went into the kitchen.

After dinner they sat on the wicker chairs and sipped coffee. The lilting strains of Mantovani played softly in the background.

Gabby had resolved not to ask about Hunter. "Did, um, anything happen after I left Washington?"

That was just the opening Henrietta needed. She looked at her daughter over the rim of her cup. "Nothing specific. It was just like being perched on the edge of a volcano, but he kept himself from erupting. In fact he was horribly polite." She made a face.

Gabby smiled and stirred her coffee uselessly. She carefully placed the spoon on the edge of the saucer. "Mother, let me ask you something."

"Certainly, dear."

"Why did you tell me that you liked my book?"

Her mother avoided meeting her eyes. "Well...." That was evidently all she planned to say.

Gabby shook her head in loving exasperation. "Because you were playing a new role? Let me see." She put her cup on the table beside her elbow and pretended to contemplate. "Was it 'loyalty to one's offspring in the face of overwhelming odds'?"

"Gabby!" her mother expostulated, trying to hide a self-conscious blush.

"Or 'anything I can do, you can do better'?" Gabby laughed sadly. "I don't know why Hunter expects me to be grown up. You never have."

Her mother looked at her with a stricken expression. "Oh, darling!" she wailed. "I hope *I* didn't have anything to do with your quarrel!"

"Don't worry about it, mother," she replied. She was infinitely tired, but she tried to inject some amusement into her smile. "Hunter and I have never gotten along."

"Are you in love with Hunter, Gabby?" Her mother caught and held her surprised gaze.

Suddenly Henrietta was all seriousness. It wouldn't be easy to lie to her, but Gabby tried anyway. "Don't be silly," she answered with asperity.

But Henrietta continued to probe until Gabby finally admitted that she might have been. "But I wrecked it all, mother. And it wasn't anybody's fault but my own. I just thought I knew more than anyone else."

"Did you know that Hunter's mother left him and his father when he was a little boy?"

"No," Gabby breathed.

Henrietta nodded. "Perhaps that explains why he's never married, never been in love. She was on her fourth husband when she died, I believe."

But he *had* been in love, for a very brief time, Gabby thought. The grief was almost more than she could stand. Hunter had meant every word he ever told her. She was the one who had ruined it all.

"He will probably never trust a woman."

"Probably not," Gabby whispered. *Not again, not after I didn't even bother to tell him that Peter Gordon was a weasel.* She remembered Hunter's face when he thought she'd gone to bed with Peter. Would she ever forget the disgust, the agony there? The picture faded to one of a young boy, anguished over the desertion of his mother. Her eyes flooded, and when Henrietta spoke again she had to blink to clear them.

"Well, to quote one of those absurd truisms you love so well," Henrietta said primly, "nothing exceeds like excess. Let time be your healer, dear. Gabby? What on earth? Are you *laughing*?"

Gabby was doubled over. The tears were only partly from the laughter that rocked her. When she caught her breath she corrected, "Nothing *succeeds* like *success*! Oh, mother! Thank you!"

GABBY'S ALOOF ACCEPTANCE of her situation set the pace for the days ahead. Surprisingly, *Captive* held its place among the top ten bestsellers. It had dropped from first place to second but had stayed solid since then.

At Nina's urging she worked on the sequel that she'd set aside while writing the ill-fated history book, but her heart wasn't in it. "What good will it do?" she asked her agent. "Hunter doesn't want it."

"Well, someone will," Nina assured her.

The work gave her something to do. She debated approaching the school board about getting her job back, but vetoed the idea the day she got her first royalty check in the mail. *Captive* had been an overwhelming financial success for her, even if it had been a personal disaster.

Two weeks went by on a snail's tread. In the third week Gabby came across a picture in the society pages of Hunter and a stunning woman, taken at a party following the opening of Broadway's newest hit. *So he's back to blondes,* she told her mirror, comparing her features to those of Hunter's date. She definitely came in second.

She had a few calls asking for magazine and newspaper interviews, but she put them off with the excuse of exhaustion after the tour, and a promise to get back to them. One man from the *New York Post* was particularly persistent. Gabby knew he wrote a gossip column in addition to the occasional feature article. She was really wary of the man, but when she finally agreed to see him she found him to be nicer than she'd expected. His name was Ron.

During the course of the interview, which took place in the park, an idea occurred to her, only to be immediately dismissed. They wandered leisurely along the pathways, Ron holding the tape recorder by a strap, Gabby with her hands in the pockets of her designer jeans.

"Has *Captive* changed your life in any way, Miss Constant?" They had been talking for more than two hours when he asked the question that sent a red-hot knife through her heart. *Yes, I'm only half alive now,* she admitted silently. *I'm in love with a man who can't be bothered with me.*

Out loud she gave a harsh painful laugh. "Call me Gabby, Ron," she told him automatically—for the third time. She let her head fall back and blinked the moisture from her eyes. The trees met over the path above them in a sun-starred canopy. "No." She met his eyes and smiled. "It hasn't changed my life, except that I no longer teach school."

"Why do I get the idea that you're lying?" he asked, not offended.

She stopped on the path and faced him. "You're right," she admitted. "But if you don't want a crying woman on your hands, we'd better shelve the subject." She turned, took two more steps. "In fact, could we shelve the rest of the interview for a few days, Ron?" Her voice had grown husky with the tears she refused to let flow.

Ron eyed her speculatively for a minute. "Will I get the rest of the story eventually?"

She should have promised anything at the moment, but her honesty made her hesitate. "I'll try," she finally offered softly.

Something of the pain that refused to dissolve must have touched the man inside the reporter. "It could mean my reputation. They sent me for a story, but...okay."

"Thanks," she whispered, crossing her arms over her stomach as if in reaction to a chill. They were covered by the sleeves of a soft blue blouse. Though it was a lovely July day, without the warmth of Hunter's love she felt frozen from the inside out.

"You're really a nice person, Gabby-Lily," Ron went on sympathetically. "And you're obviously hurting. Is it a man?"

Gabby didn't answer.

He held up his hands, palms out. "Off the record," he assured her. "Is there anything I can do to help?"

Her eyes swung to him, but she didn't see the man who stood there. The idea surfaced again. Could she? No. Why not? At least then she would know for sure.

No. It was a stupid idea. Worse than that, it probably wouldn't work.

She had spoken with Nina yesterday. Hunter had called to see if Gabby was planning to submit her next manuscript to Graham House, and to remind her agent that he wasn't interested.

It was a strange thing for him to do, almost as though he were daring her to submit so that he'd have the pleasure of rejecting her. Did he think she was a fool? She knew the answer to that, she thought wryly. But still, it was strange.

Her brow furrowed. The idea was crazy, but what harm could it do? *It could do a great deal of harm to you if it doesn't work,* she argued.

Suddenly she decided to try it. She swung to face Ron, and her eyes began to glow with the mysterious gray light for the first time in weeks. "Yes. There is something, and if it works I'll give you an exclusive preview of my next book! and... and all the interviews you want!"

He was caught in the spell of that smoky gaze and her enthusiasm, though he didn't understand it. "Great!"

"But you must promise never to reveal where you got this item."

"Item?" He was puzzled and cautious.

"Yes, for the gossip column."

"Is it true?"

Gabby blushed to the roots of her hair. "Yes, it's true. Do you promise?"

"Scout's honor." He held up two fingers.

"Cross your heart and hope to die?" she urged.

He laughed. "That, too."

She told him.

Ron had promised the item would be in the morning edition of the next day's newspaper. Gabby's mother sometimes picked up the evening edition, thank goodness.

It was almost ten o'clock before she heard the furious pounding on the outside door to her apartment.

She tucked in her pink blouse, dried her wet palms on the seat of her jeans and took a deep breath before reaching for the knob.

"You idiot! You harebrained numbskull!" Hunter erupted with all the force of a big man as he marched past her and into her small living room. He swung to face her. "What the hell are we going to do about this?" He slapped the paper he held with his other hand.

"We," not "you." Gabby's heart leaped in her breast, but she kept her voice level. "What is it, Hunter?" she asked mildly.

His dark eyes narrowed in suspicion. "Don't give

me that, Gabby! You know very well what I'm talking about.'' He held out the newspaper.

She tried to keep her expression innocent. What she wanted to do was open her arms to him. The smudges under his eyes were as dark as her own, and the lines from his nose to the corners of his mouth seemed to have deepened. But his shoulders were as broad as ever, his long thighs just as taut, and the sight of him, so virile, so handsome, turned her bones to jelly. She made herself reach out for the paper, hoping he wouldn't notice that her hands were trembling slightly.

Ron had been true to his word. The item read:

It is rumored that the beautiful (Ron had added that on his own) Gabriella Constant, a.k.a. Lily Andore, is no longer the virgin she claimed to be in a recent New Orleans interview. When this reporter called her for a comment she admitted that there was only one man who had ever fulfilled her fantasies. That's an exclusive club. Wonder who the lucky man is?

Gabby read the words silently.

''What are we going to do about it?'' Hunter repeated, his voice harsh, but certainly more calm than it had been a minute ago.

She gazed up at him. ''W-what do you mean, Hunter? The item doesn't mention you.'' Her hands were shaking badly now. She crushed the paper between them in an effort to keep them steady.

Hunter looked at her as though she'd lost her mind, but there was a soft hunger in his eyes, too, as they darted restlessly over her body. ''Your reputation, Gabby. Think what this will do to your reputation," he said huskily.

He took a step nearer, forcing her to tilt her head back if she wanted to see his face. And she did. She didn't want to miss the slightest alteration in his expression.

"It sells books," she whispered, her eyes locked into the dark depths of his. She thought he'd explode at the words.

"To hell with the damn books!" He searched her face in silence for a moment, lingering greedily on each feature. "Am I the man?" he asked finally, almost hesitantly.

"Oh, Hunter, of course you are. The only one ever. I'm sorry," she choked. "I'm so sorry I didn't trust you enough...." Her voice trailed off to a faint whisper.

"Shh, sweetheart." He reached for her then. She was folded against him in a tender, loving, forgiving embrace that brought wonderful warm tears of happiness to her eyes. His jacket was smooth under her cheek. She put up a hand to feel his rapid heartbeat.

He smelled so good, early-morning smells of after-shave and coffee. She sniffed inelegantly. "I'm sorry," she repeated in a whisper, fighting tears.

"You're going to marry me," he proclaimed softly into her hair.

"To save my reputation?" she asked.

"God, no! To save my sanity," he replied with a groan. His arms tightened, and he buried his face in her throat. "I was a jealous fool about Peter. As soon as I came to my senses I knew that you wouldn't...." He raised his head to look into her eyes. "I'd trust you with my life, Gabby, and I'll teach you to trust me. What we have is worth saving, worth working for. I've seen a lot of bad marriages, but ours won't be like that; we won't let it."

His vow was as strong and determined as the man himself, and Gabby's heart swelled to bursting with the knowledge that this commitment would be forever for both of them. "I do trust you, Hunter. I'll never doubt you again," she whispered as she lifted her face for his kiss.

"Gabriella!" A rapid knocking on the door separated them before their lips could meet. "Gabriella Constant, you open the door this minute!"

"Mother!" Gabby breathed. Her eyes revealed as much frustration as Hunter's. She pulled out of his arms, but he caught her shoulders.

"Tell me first. Do you love me?"

She shook her head helplessly. Could he not *know*? "I love you more than my life, my darling," she said firmly, expanding her answer with the adoration in her eyes.

Hunter gave a gravelly moan and covered her mouth with his. Their lips clung, craving a deeper kiss, a closer embrace, with desire that was overwhelming from being so long denied. He sighed and let her go, then crossed to open the door with an impatient wrench. "Hello, Henrietta. Come in, won't you?"

"H—Hunter?" Henrietta's was the stunned shock of complete surprise. "What...?" Her eyes sought those of her daughter, and she seemed to recover. "Gabby, Nina just called. What is this about an item in some gossip column?" She spat out the word as though it tasted bad. "What did you say in an interview in New Orleans?"

Henrietta was evidently confused. Gabby was trying to figure out a way to explain, when Hunter came to her rescue. He wrapped an arm around her shoulders and pulled her close to his side. "You don't pay any attention to gossip columnists, do you, Henrietta?"

"Why, I...well, no, of course I don't." Henrietta denied the charge vehemently.

"Well, then, forget it. I have another item. You can call Nina back and give it to her. Gabby and I are getting married. Soon."

"Married!" Henrietta scrutinized her daughter.

I'll bet I have the silliest expression on my face, thought Gabby. *Poor mother.* Suddenly she had a horrible thought. Was he doing this only to protect her? She didn't think so, but he hadn't said. She looked up at him. "D-do you have a truism for me?" she asked hesitantly.

Her mother interrupted. "Please don't start on that balderdash now, Gabby! Honestly, those silly truisms are preposterous."

But Hunter understood. He moved her around to face him and took her shoulders again in his big hands. He ignored Henrietta, except to answer her outburst with a simple, "We like them." His eyes never left Gabby's as his voice dropped to a mere whisper so that only she could hear. "Don't we?"

Gabby was unable to get any words past the lump in her throat, so she nodded hopefully.

"Here's one for you." He lifted his hands to frame her face. "Graham's law of infinity: I love you. I'll love you forever."

At first she could only see herself in his eyes, but as she watched their color deepened, and her vision went all the way into the soul of the man before her. He was finally opening himself to a hurt that she would never, ever inflict on him. "Th-that's a good one," she stammered, relief flooding through her like a tide. There need be no barriers now, not ever again.

"Self-evident and obvious. Aren't those the criteria?" he asked. His eyes were glowing with their love, and hungry. As hungry as her own.

She nodded again. "Oh, Hunter, won't you please quit talking and kiss me before I die!"

Henrietta shrugged and left them to it.

The door closed with a sharp click, the sound a signal releasing them to each other. Her arms went around his back, and she melted into him like butter on a hot biscuit.

Hunter's mouth descended, hard and hungry, to open completely over her parted lips. His tongue thrust deep into her mouth, branding her forever as his alone. The hands that had framed her face, moved across her shoulders and down her back to her hips. He lifted her until she felt the pressure of his arousal.

A moan, animal-like, escaped from somewhere in her throat, surprising her, but she had no time to dwell on its origin. She and Hunter were together in the eye of a storm, a whirlwind of longing, and that was all that mattered to her at this moment. They were together. The tears that she had fought so valiantly during the tense moments earlier, now flowed with warm release, wetting her cheeks.

He felt them and misunderstood their cause. "Sweetheart, don't cry. Oh, God, don't cry." Instantly the hands at her back were moving in concern, restless and impassioned still, but caring. She thought she had never welcomed anything as she did the touch of those hands. She wanted to know them everywhere. And her own were just as busy, tracing the band of muscle at his waist, reaching up to reacquaint themselves with the nape of his neck, the width of his shoulders and down to his flat hips. "I've missed you so. Oh, Hunter, I've missed you. I'm crying because I'm happy, don't you know that?" she confided.

"You're crazy," he told her tenderly. His arms tightened briefly, and then he swung her up with breathcatching swiftness. "Where's your bedroom?" he growled against her throat. "I can comfort you better in there. Preferably on your back and naked."

"That way." She indicated the hall with a limp wave of her wrist, all the while covering as much of his cheek as she could reach with kisses. "But I haven't made the bed."

"Good!" He stopped to give her another burning kiss.

"Hurry!" she commanded when she could breathe again. Her voice was weak and husky.

Hunter dropped her to the mattress from a precarious height and she bounced. Grandmother's poor bed gave a protesting groan.

Before she came down from the second bounce he had shed the blazer and pulled the knit shirt fiercely over his head, rumpling his hair.

"I was afraid you weren't coming over," she said as she got to her knees to help with his belt buckle. "It was getting so late." Her fingers were fumbling and clumsy in her haste, but finally she had the belt free.

He let her worry about his zipper and started to work on the buttons of her blouse. "I overslept this morning. You're not wearing a bra," he murmured.

She smiled at the endearing way the two incongruous statements were delivered in the same moderate but hurried tone. The pink fabric was peeled expertly off her shoulders and tossed across the room to join his shirt in a crumpled heap in a corner.

"Are you having trouble sleeping, too? I—"

"And eating, and walking around, and breathing," he interrupted. "Later, my little tiger." At last he managed to free the metal button at her waist. "Later," he mumbled hoarsely as he dumped her backward on the bed and pulled the jeans away. She levered her hips slightly when he reached for the scrap of lace that was her panties. Soon they, too, fell on the growing collection on the floor and were covered in seconds by the rest of his clothes.

He stood by the bed for a long moment like some magnificent reincarnation of a Greek god. Only his eyes moved, devouring her shape with deeply moving hunger and a remnant of desperation.

"It's been so long. I *need* you, Gabby," he grated hoarsely. Moving slowly, he brought one knee down on the bed beside her. Then Hunter leaned forward, his hands flat on either side of her head, to search her features; and for the first time since he'd arrived he allowed her to see just how profoundly the pain had ravaged him—how the suffering that had become part of his life for the past few weeks had left its mark.

Gabby recognized the anguish in his expression. She had faced it in her own mirror every day. She

wanted to cry out at the sight, which twisted like a
knife in her heart. In their fear to trust they had
wounded each other deeply. Now it was time to
salve the wounds, to heal with the only effective
remedy available to them—their love. At this moment their spiritual ache was as intense as the physical one; the wonder of knowing that they belonged
together was as necessary as their pleasurable excitement. She held out her arms. "I need you every
bit as much, if not more, my darling," she told him.

He reached for her with trembling hands. "Please,
please, don't ever leave me again," he finished on a
whisper.

Her voice was as quiet as his had been, but steady
and firm in its determination. "I'll never leave you,
my dearest love. Never."

The moment of vulnerability was over almost as
quickly as it had begun. All at once his lips were at
her throat, his hands on her breasts, kneading and
squeezing the sensitive flesh, plucking gently at her
nipples, pushing the soft mounds together to form a
cleavage to harbor his damp tongue as he moved
down her body. He seemed ravenous for the taste of
her skin. His breath was moist when he shifted his
mouth to the pink tips, laving and sucking until they
shone wetly and bloomed with erotic desire.

Gabby responded with unrestrained sensuality,
arching her back to give him more of herself, to
demand more of him. Bold with desire her hands
slid down his stomach to find the heat of his passion.

He gave an aggressive growl and loomed over her,
spreading her legs almost roughly with one of his
knees. His hands stroked the inside of her thighs up-

ward to the moist warm cradle of her femininity, teasing her with his knowing fingers until she was writhing, begging him to make her complete. She yearned to feel him inside her, to move with him as one person.

It was not a gentle coming together. Only Hunter's determination that she be satisfied curbed his impatience. Speech was impossible, so she met his eyes in an effort to communicate her love without words.

He moved within her, slowly at first, never releasing her gaze; then the tension began to build, increasing his rhythm and thrust, until they both caught their breath for an endless, wonderful moment, poised on the precipice of the ultimate experience of a man and woman. The climactic convulsions ripped through them simultaneously, and they clung to each other as the only steady spots in a world racked and tumbling with all the force of an earthquake.

The aftermath left them both gasping, their bodies tangled and moist with perspiration.

When their hearts had returned to a fairly normal beat, Hunter propped himself on his elbows and tenderly pushed the damp hair away from her brow. His lips played over her eyes, her cheeks, her nose, until they finally met hers in a deep, fervent kiss that was as much an enduring vow as were his words of love.

He lifted his head, and in his eyes was an expression that she'd never seen there before, not even when he'd first told her that he loved her.

He'd always been confident. In fact, his assurance in any situation was one of the things that used to annoy her because of the slight tinge of arrogance that colored it. She realized the arrogance had been a form of defense. There was none in his face now. This confidence was that of a man who looked to the future, knowing it held everything he desired. "I love you," he said quietly. "I love you more than anything in the world. Having you for my wife will make my life complete."

"Oh, Hunter," she whispered softly and smiled. She lifted her hands to thread her fingers into the blackness of his hair. Her eyes feasted on each part of his face as she traced the features lovingly, across a thick brow, down the side of his straight nose, lingering last and for a long time at his mouth.

Suddenly she thought of something. "I have a confession to make." She hesitated. "But I want you to know that I did... what I did because I love you so much and I didn't know what else...."

He chuckled and dipped his head to stifle her words with a prolonged kiss. Then he rolled to his side, keeping her in the circle of his arms. His chin rested on the top of her head. "You're very serious. What is it, sweetheart?"

It was easier this way, not having to look at him. She ran her palm across his strong hand before she answered. "Do you promise not to be angry?"

"How can I promise that?" he asked reasonably.

She thought about the question for a moment. "Well, remember... you've proposed and I've accepted, and if you don't want a breach of promise suit...."

"Gabriella." His voice held a hint of warning now, and she could feel the muscles tense under her cheek and hand.

"Oh, all right. I'm the one who gave the item to

the gossip columnist," she said hurriedly and held her breath.

Without warning she was flipped onto her back, and he loomed above her once again. However, she noted in relief, the gleam in the black eyes wasn't anger but affectionate amusement.

"I figured that out," he informed her smugly.

"You did?" He nodded. "And you aren't furious?" She couldn't believe her good luck.

"Darling, I was relieved." His arms slipped under her back, gathering her closer. The brush of hair against her breasts began to ignite the familiar flames within her body, and she moved her face for an expected kiss. But it didn't come. Instead he went on, "I had almost given up on your submitting another manuscript to Graham House, and I couldn't figure out how to get across this barrier between us."

"What?" Her brow furrowed. She didn't understand. She pushed against his chest, needing a little space to think but he wouldn't relinquish his hold. "You told Nina not to dare submit anything to you," she accused shakily.

"Of course I did. I wasn't going to let you think you could walk over me and get away with it."

His figurative swagger was back, as annoying as ever. She snorted. "Typical masculine reasoning."

"Yep," he admitted without a trace of remorse. One hand had worked its way up her back and now held her head still for the kisses he bestowed in the spot below her ear, on her temple, at the corner of her mouth. "But I missed you. I felt I had lost a part of myself when you left Washington."

She didn't doubt his sincerity, but was not to be

distracted so easily. "You recovered quickly enough. I saw your picture in the paper last week with one of your ever present blondes."

"It didn't mean a thing," he said, dismissing with cavalier disregard the woman who had caused Gabby such heartache. "I did it to make you jealous. You're the only important woman in my life."

Gabby felt like screaming in frustration. "If you felt that way why did you let me go *through* this? Didn't it ever occur to you to simply call?" she snapped. She was trying to control her temper, but it was becoming harder by the minute.

He ignored her outburst. "Your eyes turn the most beautiful color when you're angry. Sort of like smoky silver. I was planning to come to the Saturday soirée this weekend to see what kind of reception I got."

"Well, *I* wouldn't have been there," she informed him sharply. "I hate those things."

He went on in the same careless tone, as though she hadn't spoken. "Do you know that before today you never told me that you loved me, Gabriella."

In the well of silence that followed the mild indictment Gabby caught her breath. She remembered before he had opened the door to admit her mother he'd asked in that same almost throwaway tone if she loved him. And she'd been shocked that he hadn't known.

He'd been as unsure as she had! The Great Hunter Graham had been uncertain of a woman's love because of a legacy from an uncaring mother. Someday they would have to talk about his mother, but not today. She refused to let another woman intrude on this moment.

Then she recalled the things he'd said in Washington. "But when I apologized you said Lily was more trouble than she was worth," she offered tentatively. "I thought you didn't care anymore."

He sighed a deep shuddering sigh and buried his face in the soft curve of her neck as though openly seeking reassurance at last. "Darling, I had to learn to trust, too," he finally confessed. "I've never been able to put much faith in a woman before you. That first night, when we went dancing?" He raised his head, and a brow, in question.

She nodded silently, not wanting to break into his confidence.

"I think I fell in love with your honesty that night. You didn't play coy games. You were as refreshing as a spring breeze. I tried to tell myself I didn't want to get involved, but it was probably inevitable from that point that you were mine. And then as the tour progressed you seemed to change. I wanted the scruffy, outspoken Gabby back, the maddening child who needed me to rescue her. But she had turned into the worldly wise Lily who didn't need anyone."

"You created a monster." Slender arms crept up to his neck. "Gabby and Lily will always love you and need you, Hunter. You'll never have reason to doubt that."

He searched her eyes, and further, into her very being. "I believe you," he declared. Then his face blotted out all light as he began to kiss her again, this time letting the passion build in slow, languorous stages.

HUNTER'S MASSIVE CHEST shook with the chuckle that worked its way out. Gabby tilted her head back against his shoulder to scan his features with a quizzical smile.

"What's funny?"

"Us. You and me." He stretched luxuriously. "It will never be boring."

She wiggled her toes against the bare calf of his leg. "No," she agreed. "But we'll probably have some royal battles."

"No, we won't. When we're married you are going to control that damnable temper, Gabriella, because I have no intention of putting up with your tantrums." He shook his head in exasperation.

Was he teasing? She thought he was, but even so he couldn't be allowed to get away with such a dictatorial pronouncement. She grabbed a handful of hair on his chest and pulled. "Me? What about your arrogance?"

"Ouch!" He squeezed her hand until she released her hold. "That hurt." He sighed his complaint. "When I think of the women who would have killed for this chance...and all of them, as you so kindly reminded me, gorgeous blondes."

Gabby sat straight up. What a horrible thing to say! Especially at a time like this! Her mouth was open to protest, but then she closed it again. A sudden suspicion lit a gleam in her eye and curved her mouth in a smile as she looked back over her shoulder at the exasperating man she loved, his hands now folded complacently under his head.

"Are you testing me?" she said after a moment.

"You see?" He acknowledged the accusation with a satisfied grin. "You *can* control yourself when you try."

She sighed, thinking what an interesting marriage this was going to be, with her temper and his pride. "I'm learning." She leaned down to touch her lips softly to his chin and shifted her legs, untangling them. Slowly she rose, enjoying his warm gaze on her naked body without a trace of self-consciousness. Making her movements as graceful as possible, she crossed the room to open the closet and reached for a robe.

"Where are you going?" he asked finally, as she had known he would.

"To use the telephone." She slid her arms into the sleeves of the rose silk wrap and belted it at her waist.

"The telephone?" He stirred restlessly on the bed and sat up. "What the hell is so important that you have to make a call right now?"

Moving toward the open doorway she tugged at the belt, tightening it further. She knew that the action defined her breasts quite provocatively. "I have to call Jacques and Marie...to see if they can turn me into a gorgeous blonde."

He caught her at the door to the kitchen. "Uncle, uncle," he murmured, his breath warming her nape as he pushed the heavy mane aside. "Don't you dare change a hair on this beautiful head. I love it exactly as it is, temper and all." He turned her in his arms.

The kiss they shared was deliciously suffocating. It threatened to dissolve every bone in Gabby's body. Her head was spinning wildly before it was over, and she had to cling to him to remain upright.

"Let's fly to Jamaica this afternoon," he muttered urgently against her wet, swollen lips. "You can get married there in twenty-four hours."

"What a wonderful idea," she answered without hesitation, though she was dazed and disoriented. "And the way I'm feeling now, I won't even need a plane."

Harlequin Stationery Offer

Personalized Rainbow Memo Pads for you or a friend

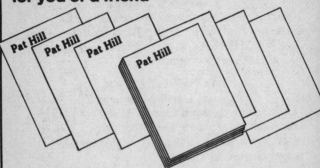

Picture your name in bold type at the top of these attractive rainbow memo pads. Each 4¼″ x 5½″ pad contains 150 rainbow sheets—yellow, pink, gold, blue, buff and white—enough to last you through months of memos. Handy to have at home or office.

Just clip out three proofs of purchase (coupon below) from an August or September release of Harlequin Romance, Harlequin Presents, Harlequin Superromance, Harlequin American Romance, Harlequin Temptation or Harlequin Intrigue and add $4.95 (includes shipping and handling), and we'll send you *two* of these attractive memo pads imprinted with your name.

- -

Harlequin Stationery Offer

(PROOF OF PURCHASE)

NAME_____

(Please Print)

ADDRESS_____

CITY_____STATE_____ZIP_____

NAME ON STATIONERY_____

Mail 3 proofs of purchase, plus check or money order for $4.95 payable to:	Harlequin Books P.O. Box 52020 Phoenix, AZ 85072	5-3 STAT-1

Offer expires December 31, 1984. (Not available in Canada)

Introducing
Harlequin Intrigue

Because romance can be quite an adventure

Available in August wherever paperbacks are sold.

INT-3

INTRODUCING

Harlequin Temptation _{T.M.}

Sensuous...contemporary...compelling...reflecting today's love relationships! The passionate torment of a woman torn between two loves...the siren call of a career ...the magnetic advances of an impetuous employer–nothing is left unexplored in this romantic new series from Harlequin. You'll thrill to a candid new frankness as men and women seek to form lasting relationships in the face of temptations that threaten true love. *Don't miss a single one!* You can start new *Harlequin Temptation* coming to your home each month for just $1.75 per book–a saving of 20¢ off the suggested retail price of $1.95. Begin with your FREE copy of *First Impressions*. Mail the reply card today!

First Impressions
by Maris Soule

He was involved with her best friend! Tracy Dexter couldn't deny her attraction to her new boss. Mark Prescott looked more like a jet set playboy than a high school principal–and he acted like one, too. It wasn't right for Tracy to go out with him, not when her friend Rose had already staked a claim. It wasn't right, even though Mark's eyes were so persuasive, his kiss so probing and intense. Even though his hands scorched her body with a teasing, raging fire...and when he gently lowered her to the floor she couldn't find the words to say no.

A word of warning to our regular readers: While Harlequin books are always in good taste, you'll find more sensuous writing in new *Harlequin Temptation* than in other Harlequin romance series.

® ™Trademarks of Harlequin Enterprises Ltd.

Exclusive Harlequin home subscriber benefits!

- SPECIAL LOW PRICES for home subscribers only
- CONVENIENCE of home delivery
- NO CHARGE for postage and handling
- FREE *Harlequin Romance Digest*®
- FREE BONUS books
- NEW TITLES 2 months ahead of retail
- MEMBER of the largest romance fiction book club in the world

GET FIRST IMPRESSIONS FREE
Harlequin Temptation ™

Mail to: **HARLEQUIN READER SERVICE**

In the U.S.A.
2504 West Southern Avenue
Tempe, AZ 85282

In Canada
P.O. Box 2800, Postal Station A
5170 Yonge Street,
Willowdale, Ont. M2N 5T5

YES, please send me FREE and **without obligation** my *Harlequin Temptation* romance novel, *First Impressions*. If you do not hear from me after I have examined my FREE book, please send me 4 new *Harlequin Temptation* novels each month as soon as they come off the press. I understand that I will be billed only $1.75 per book (total $7.00)–a saving of 20¢ off the suggested retail price of $1.95. There are no shipping and handling or any other hidden charges. There is no minimum number of books that I have to purchase. In fact, I may cancel this arrangement at any time. *First Impressions* is mine to keep as a free gift, even if I do not buy any additional books.

Name

Address   Apt. No.

City   State/Prov.   Zip/Postal Code

Signature (If under 18, parent or guardian must sign.)

This offer is limited to one order per household and not valid to present *Harlequin Temptation* subscribers. We reserve the right to exercise discretion in granting membership. Offer expires December 31, 1984

® ™ Trademarks of Harlequin Enterprises Ltd.   T-SUB-2X